DOCTORS' DAUGHTERS

The arrival of the new bishop at Mitrebury and his orders for all clergy to take up jogging and a diet of boiled rice sends the men of the cloth scurrying to the Old Chapterhouse Surgery for sick notes. The vastly overworked doctors fear they might even have to cancel their afternoon golf to meet the demand! This is simply not on, so when they learn that two of their friends now have qualified doctors as children, they seize their opportunity to escape – of course it never occurred to any of them that these valiant new doctors might be women...

DOCTORS' DAUGHTERS

DOCTORS' DAUGHTERS

by

Richard Gordon

Dales Large Print Books
Long Preston, North Yorkshire,
BD23 4ND, England.

British Library Cataloguing in Publication Data.

Gordon, Richard
    Doctors' daughters.

    A catalogue record of this book is
    available from the British Library

    ISBN   1-84262-377-X pbk

Dales Large Print is an imprint of Library Magna Books Ltd.

Printed and bound in Great Britain by
T.J. (International) Ltd., Cornwall, PL28 8RW

To
Our Doctors' Daughters

1

The city of Mitrebury wore the twentieth century like a coat of paint.

For six hundred years, its cathedral's spire had hopefully pointed Englishmen the way to Heaven. On its grassy close below, a knot of oaks had been gathered in solemn deliberation since the death of Queen Anne. In the massive shadow of its sanctity, cobbled lanes tangled among houses with gnarled chimney-pots, their windows and doors askew like old men's teeth, the brickwork patterned like the ancient lines on rock.

These buildings housed placid generations steadfast in the service of God. Only one strove for beneficial results in this world rather than the next.

A plate polished to the inscrutability of the cathedral's mediaeval brasses announced to the assiduous reader,

The Old Chapterhouse Surgery
Dr Carmichael, Dr Hill & Dr Fellows-Smith
8.00 to 9.00 – 5.00 to 6.00

Nobody in Mitrebury knew why it was called 'The Old Chapterhouse Surgery.' Not even Archdeacon Bellwether, who had charge of the parsonages, and the parish churches from crypt to crocket. There *was* a chapterhouse, but it was demolished by Oliver Cromwell's cannon-balls in the summer of 1643, which in Mitrebury was the other afternoon. The truth was simple. The founders of the practice, almost forty years ago, had thought the name sounded rather well.

Towards one o'clock on a bright, gusty day which had the Mitrebury weather-vanes wagging like the tails of excited dogs, two of these doctors were in clinical conference.

'No hope for her,' said Dr Freddie Fellows-Smith gloomily. He was bald, bulky, in gingery tweeds and a canary waistcoat with foxes' head buttons. 'Poor thing.'

'Very sad.' Dr 'Biggin' Hill's striped tie and blazer with *Per Ardua ad Astra* crest proclaimed lifelong pride in the RAF, in which he had served the war as medical officer to the big WAAF depot in Morecambe, Lancs. 'When's she likely to prang?'

'Any day. She's just wasting away.'

'What's your diagnosis?'

'The dreaded red stomach worm.'

With a No 5 iron, Biggin chipped an NHS plastic pillbox across the surgery sitting-room into the wicker wastepaper basket.

It was past the third Sunday in Lent, when Mitrebury felt against its cheek the timorous antennae of spring. The chestnut buds bulged like treacle toffee, the catkins hung like jaundiced caterpillars, the woods twinkled with primroses and the daffodils showed exactly why Wordsworth became so excited. The softer air wrapped the sickly survivors of winter as blankets those of a shipwreck, and the morning chorus of coughing in the waiting-room was muted.

'May be psychological?' Biggin suggested hopefully.

Freddie shook his head morosely, tugging the gold blocked, slim spine of William Harvey's famous sixteenth-century work *De Motu Cordis*. This released a section of shelves filled with medical books, which covered one wall. The remaining decorations were a glass case of silver cups he had won at the Mitrebury Agricultural Show, and another with a pheasant he had long ago shot and casseroled. He reached among the bottles within the concealed cupboard, and poured himself a pink gin.

'How many little ones has she?' asked Biggin sympathetically.

'Nine. Even a diet of treacle and bran mash didn't work. Pinkers?'

'Roger,' Biggin accepted.

'I've decided to do her in. As mercifully as possible, of course.' Freddie sprinkled ango-stura. 'So if you want a side of bacon, call at my farm next week and collect.'

The sitting-room door opened, as the third partner returned from his morning rounds.

Dr Roland Carmichael was tall, handsome and grey-haired. He felt that three divorces allowed him to dress in flowered shirts and boutique suits, like a successful actor. He refused a drink. He sprawled wearily in a leather arm-chair which appeared to have already finished one useful lifetime in some Pall Mall club.

'Got a brace of wood-pigeon for you in the car,' Freddie told him, leaning against the marble fireplace. 'They make a passable stew with plenty of thyme and marjoram.'

Roland thanked him curtly.

'Got to fill your wifeless larder, eh?' Freddie continued genially. 'Though they're rather full of shot, I'm afraid. Like that rabbit last

14

week. I had to pepper him heavily from the south-east while he was proceeding north-west. And the ptarmigan – not left hanging too long?'

Roland told him it was edible.

'I say, old man, are you feeling quite A1?' asked Biggin Hill with concern.

'Of course I am,' Roland replied impatiently. 'I'm as fit as a man – as a boy,' he corrected himself, 'half my age.'

They had been students together at St Boniface's Hospital in London, and like Englishmen who had known one another in youth, trundled through life in a protective packing of chaff. They were the same age, which allowed the others to tease Roland rumbustiously over his anxiety at not showing it.

Freddie confided, sipping his gin, 'To my professional eye, you look as likely to drop off the hook as that ptarmigan did.'

'I'm as healthy as a teetotal, athletic monk on a diet,' Roland assured him forcefully.

'Perhaps that's your trouble?' Biggin suggested mildly. 'As the only one of us not currently married, you should be in bed with a skilful nurse.'

'Since we started this practice, I've recognized you two as a pair of hypochondriacs. I refuse to suffer from it now, second-hand.' Roland Carmichael rose and strode from the room.

The waiting room outside was oak-panelled, its decorations a stag's head, a huge salmon in a glass case and a shiny Farmers' Union calendar. The patients could wait on four richly-carved pews, bought cheaply by Freddie at a village auction when a thunder-storm had ruined his afternoon's fishing. These were strewn with tattered copies of the *Field*, *Country Life*, the *Stockbreeder* and some seed catalogues. At an antique desk just inside the front door sat the only resident of the building.

'Doctor – your evening surgery appointments.' Mr Windows held out a pencilled list. He was a leather faced man in a short white coat, bearing the dignity of a first-class steward aboard a cruise liner – from which Freddie had enticed him ashore as caretaker. In the way events effortlessly evolved in the practice, he had since risen to become receptionist, secretary, nurse and in his own estimation spare doctor.

Roland squinted at arm's length.

'If I may make so bold to diagnose,' Mr Windows suggested, 'ain't it time you started wearing glasses?'

16

'Thank you very much! My vision is perfectly normal. Sixth-sixths. The last time I tested it.'

'If you ask me, doctor, you got the ingrowing arcus senilis.'

'Why is everyone pestering me this morning about my health?' Roland disappeared into one of the three consulting-rooms, slamming the door.

In the sitting-room, Biggin snapped open a case and extracted his stethoscope. 'I'm going to get old Roland in the gun-sights,' he announced firmly.

'What if he refuses to take his trousers down?' Freddie unclasped his own slim leather case, and began thoughtfully to assemble a shotgun. 'You can hardly court-martial him. You were demobilized in 1946. Remember?'

Biggin strode into the consulting room, finding the doctor in shirtsleeves, nervously taking his blood-pressure.

'What's the reading?' Biggin enquired.

'Three hundred over one-fifty.'

'What!'

'Oh, rather less...' Roland squinted at the scale beside the column of mercury. 'They mark instruments in such small figures these days.'

17

His sigh synchronized with the escaping air which hissed from the black inflatable cuff round his biceps. 'You're right, Biggin,' he admitted. 'I've been a bit off-colour recently. A hotchpotch of symptoms. Belly-ache and headache. Weakness and lassitude. A foul taste in my mouth. It started about the time Charlotte and I split up last year. You know how doctors hate admitting they're ill? It's like Sherlock Holmes finding his Baker Street flat burgled.'

Biggin clapped his shoulder. 'Chocks away. On the couch.'

The examination of one doctor by another is an encounter as delicate as a poker game between two card sharpers. The doctor on his feet politely confesses total ignorance of medicine compared with the doctor on his back, who is equally civilly struggling to hide his abject terror of the consultation.

Dr Biggin Hill's clinical experience with the RAF, as medical officer to the Mitrebury police and racecourse, to several hunts and mountaineering clubs – he seemed dis-appointed by a holiday in which no one broke a leg – had left him with an invigor-ating bedside manner. Laying a hand on Roland's bare abdomen, he shouted through the open door, 'I say, Freddie. Come and

18

have a feel of this.'

Freddie wandered in, gun under arm. He prodded. 'Kidney.'

'Spleen,' objected Biggin.

'My dear fellow,' Freddie said scathingly. 'A first year medical student with a hangover could tell you that's kidney.'

'I suspect, Freddie, you would only recognize a kidney if it was served with bacon for your breakfast,' Biggin responded icily.

'Will you please discuss my internal organs with proper respect?' Roland interrupted.

Biggin looked hurt. 'It's for your own good.'

'That's what you tell the patients,' Roland objected sourly.

'You are a patient,' Freddie reminded him. 'However socially disastrous. It's the size of a coconut,' he decided, still prodding.

'I thought more a Golden Delicious,' Biggin disagreed.

'It's my abdomen, not a fruit-barrow,' Roland pointed out.

'Perhaps it's malaria?' Biggin suggested. 'Did you go to the tropics for your summer holidays?'

'You know perfectly well that I went to Devon. For a month on a health farm.'

'Oh, you can pick up all sorts of nasty

things in those places,' Biggin assured him. 'We must do blood tests. Mr Windows! Syringe, magnum size.'

Roland wriggled. 'You also know perfectly well that I've got a neurosis about being at the wrong end of sharp needles.'

'Mind if I have a grope, doctors?' Mr Windows appeared with a large syringe. 'I've said for weeks the poor doctor was proper pathological.'

'Feel free,' Freddie invited generously.

'Glanders,' decided Mr Windows, hand on bare flesh.

'In that case, we'd better saddle him,' said Biggin. 'You get it in horses. Just a little prick. Won't feel a thing.'

'That's something else you tell the patients,' Roland snapped. The needle went in. He yelled.

Archdeacon Bellwether froze on the surgery doorstep. 'Some poor soul,' he muttered apprehensively. 'Perhaps in mortal agony.'

He pulled the bell. Its cracked clang affected him like a bell-buoy some worried mariner in a rocky coast. As he pushed open the front door, another yell came from the consulting room. He shut it quickly, concerned that a river of blood might flow across the surgery floor, causing him vulgarly to faint. He stood with hands clasped in the broad forecourt, pondering that God in His infinite wisdom must have good reason to vouchsafe him such a miserable morning – but it was some reason beyond himself.

2

When the Old Chapterhouse Surgery had started practice at eight o'clock that morning, Mr Bellwether was sitting on a small blue plastic chair in the hallway of the bishop's palace, reflecting on changes in the Church of England since the times of the Victorian novelist Anthony Trollope.

Anthony Trollope's Archdeacon Grantly, of Plumstead in Barsetshire, was shamelessly rich. The Grantly property in *The Last Chronicle of Barset* extended into the neighbouring parishes of Eiderdown and Stopingum, with fifteen hundred acres to be shot over by his son the Major. Mr Bellwether was shamefully poor.

Archdeacon Grantly was a powerful nuisance in the cathedral city of Barchester. He himself detested the slightest fuss in Mitrebury.

Trollope's archdeacon indulged an odd abomination of circular dinner-tables, Mr Bellwether remembered, as fit only for dissenters and calico-printers. Mr Bellwether and his wife often supped at the kitchen dinette, now he had taken a small modern house on the unfashionable London side of the city, after his official residence in the precincts had tumbled down.

The palace filled the west end of the cathedral close, a monument to episcopal dignity seemingly constructed from huge blocks of milk fudge. The top floor now housed the bishop, the rest a dozen bodies busy over the spiritual, moral or social good of their fellow humans.

The vast entrance hall, through which eighty bishops had shuttled to the temporal world, was now a waiting room for the departments which the latest one had crammed into the old building. The wormy panelling was replaced by washable pink plastic. The undulating oak floor was superseded with hard-wearing beige carpeting. It was already full.

Young women with raucous, pugnacious children waited for the Single Parent Guidance Unit, which would piously take these off their hands for several delightful hours. An old man bubbling into an empty pipe wanted the Senior Citizens Art Appreciation Group, which offered free coach trips with sit-down lunch. Separated from the archdeacon by a rubber plant were two youths released even earlier that morning from Mitrebury jail, where the bishop's palace was renowned for the cash value of its rehabilitation.

Archdeacon Grantly would never have sat in a waiting room, Mr Bellwether meditated. Nor would Mrs Proudie ever have countenanced in her husband's Barchester palace those dreadful stackable plastic chairs.

Five storeys above, the bishop was sitting at the plain desk of his bare, businesslike study, as unsparingly energetic as usual.

'Good morning, my lord.' His domestic chaplain had entered, as discreetly as a winter shadow.

'*Do* call me Peter,' the bishop invited.

'Forgive me. Old habits die painfully. The old bishop was so strict on etiquette.'

'The last bishop, God rest his soul, was born almost forty years before I was. Into a social solar system separated from ours by astronomical distances. We must not confuse good manners with mere mannerisms, Arthur.'

'Of course not, Peter.' The chaplain crossed the chessboard floor of plastic tiles. He was short, fat and pale, with a sharp nose and round glasses. His thick black hair gleamed like his stout black shoes, his heavy, worn dark suit was laboriously pressed, his clerical collar seemed enamelled.

'If the Church doesn't come to terms with current social usages, humanity will find one more excuse for refusing to take notice of us,' the bishop continued affably. He worried daily at seeming offensive to the Reverend Arthur Dawney. The bishop was incapable of hating any man, but there were some he wished held preferments in the missionary field. 'I can assure you, I'm conscious enough of my own importance without needing a reminder each time I'm spoken to.'

'I hope you don't find me lacking in respect?' asked the chaplain, who did not care how offensive he was.

'That was a joke.'

'Ah! I see. The late bishop seldom made jokes.' The chaplain laid on the desk the bishop's morning sheaf of letters. His pudgy pink fingers reminded the bishop of cocktail sausages, with which, as a sociable man, he was uncensoriously familiar. 'Mr Bellwether is downstairs.'

The bishop raised his thick, sandy confulent eyebrows. 'I cannot keep an archdeacon waiting.'

A few moments later, the bishop was

greeting him, 'Good morning, Bill.'

'Good morning, Peter.' Mr Bellwether was large, middle-aged, easygoing and adaptable. Had the bishop required to be addressed as 'Me old china,' he would have complied. He sat in another uncomfortable chair, one sombrely-clad leg over another. 'Good to see you back. You must tell me all about America.'

'It was fascinating,' the bishop said warmly. 'America has so much which appeals to me. The generosity. The enthusiasm. The informality. Janet will have all our transparencies developed tomorrow. Why don't you and Mary come round and spend the evening?'

'I don't think we can manage tomorrow,' said the archdeacon firmly.

'Those she took of the Grand Canyon are most impressive.'

'It's very big, I believe?'

'*Very* big.' This seemed to end their conversation. The bishop swivelled in his black plastic office chair. 'We can learn much from the Americans. About health, for instance.'

The archdeacon was instantly suspicious. 'I am very well, thank you.'

The bishop fixed him with a steely eye. 'You will shortly be much better.'

Peter Ivens, the Right Reverend the Lord

Bishop of Mitrebury, was a little past forty. His appointment by the Prime Minister had caused umbrage at the Athenaeum Club in London, contention in the *Church Times*, and outright laughter at All Souls College, Oxford, which for five hundred years had seen itself as an episcopal finishing-school. Mr Bellwether had reflected mildly that the bishops seemed to be getting younger every year, like the lady Wimbledon champions.

Peter Ivens was tall, lissom, handsome, with thick ginger hair, frank blue eyes and pink cheeks. He had played rugby for Oxford, cricket for England and karate for fun. Strong minded and sharp witted, he was a smooth manipulator of men and events, and clever enough to appear politically stupid. He was worshipped by newspaper reporters, because he always thought hard for a neat quote, which saved them the bother of thinking at all. Gossip-columnists cherished his seemly eccentricities, a bishop found in a pub equalling a pop star found in a sexual orgy. Constantly on the chat shows, he had stamped his personality on a British public which has a vague, inbred awareness of bishops. Or something like his personality. He knew wisely television to be as treacherous as Snow White's stepmother's mirror on the wall.

'*Mens sana in corpore sano.*' The bishop returned through the window the stony gaze of the saints clustered round the cathedral's great west door. 'Jogging! All America does it.' The archdeacon became gravely worried. 'A healthy Church demands healthy church-men. We must set an example. Why should the Devil have all the good commercials?'

Physical exercise had not before come into the archdeacon's consideration. His game at Oxford was chess. His wife mowed their small lawn while he pruned their few roses. 'I'm rather past the age–'

'You're precisely the age that *needs* exercise.' The bishop struck him vigorously on the shoulder. 'Lose some "flab", eh? My father tells me Field-Marshal Montgomery sent all officers under the rank of brigadier on a weekly cross-country run. Why, it'll be tremendous fun, Bill! Meet here tomorrow morning at seven.'

Alarm in the archdeacon turned to horror. He was a busy man, who collected commit-tees as others collect stamps. Seven was his only voluptuous moment of the day, when he could lie in bed with his cup of tea, stare at the ceiling and think of nothing. There would be photographers, even television.

How they would laugh in Canterbury! He searched wildly for an objection, and hit on an unanswerable one. 'I have no footer shorts.'

'I have a good supply of track suits. With luminous stripes down the sides. And another thing—'

The bishop seemed to glow more radiantly with health and holiness. What devilish scheme has the man in mind? the archdeacon wondered irritably. The bishop had shown a disturbing interest in the Mitrebury municipal baths. The archdeacon loathed swimming, which he found too cold, public and wet. Potholing? Roller skating? Not parachuting? he thought in panic.

'My arduous investigations under the burning sun of India, during your last snowy winter, greatly affected me,' the bishop revealed. He always returned from his pilgrimages glittering with bright ideas, Mr Bellwether remembered uncomfortably.

'Here in Mitrebury,' he continued, 'we have water on tap, drains beneath our floors. If we want abundant and cheap raiment, we have but to visit Marks and Spencer's. We do not drive our bullock to the plough all day, and warm ourselves from a fire of its dung all night.'

The archdeacon agreed with him.

'In India, I had eyes to see, and a nose to smell. It is hypocritical, uttering platitudes about the Third World from our pulpits and on television. We must *feel* what it's like to be an untouchable sitting on his charpoy in his dhoti beside the Ganges. I desire the Mitrebury clergy to live on rice and water during the remainder of Lent. You may add a little milk, if you wish. Preferably goat's.'

The archdeacon gulped. *'Fridays* in Lent?' he asked hopefully.

'Oh, that wouldn't have any impact on the media at all,' the bishop told him authoritatively. 'We'll have an all-night vigil or two,' he mused. 'The BBC will be no trouble, and I think I'll get ITV if I throw in choral evensong as well. Now you must excuse me, Bill. So much work accumulated while in the States.' He picked the top letter on his desk. 'H'm, they want me in Australia and New Zealand next winter. I feel it my duty to accept. I often wonder what St Paul might have achieved, had he the advantages of air travel. As I keep impressing on the dean and chapter, Christ was a great communicator. I see Canada is interested in me, too,' he murmured with satisfaction.

Descending the stairs with the chaplain

from his own small office outside, the archdeacon sighed deeply.

'Do you recall a remark of the late Sir John Leslie, the author who died some ten years ago? "The ideal of the English Church has been to provide a resident gentleman for every parish in the Kingdom." Our ideals seem to have grown as complicated as everything else in modern life.'

The chaplain responded primly. 'The bishop believes that change is the only challenge which resolute men refuse.'

'I suppose you're jogging tomorrow morning?'

'Oh, no.'

The archdeacon turned a fishy eye. 'And why not?' A smile spread across the chaplain's smooth pale face, like melting lard. He tapped his breastbone energetically. 'The old ticker.'

'But you're as healthy as a horse.'

'Not at all. Appearances belie me. I suffered rheumatism in childhood. Or so I am told. Violent exercise would probably kill me stone dead.'

'You got the bishop to believe that?' the archdeacon asked incredulously.

'The bishop had no option,' the chaplain replied smugly. 'I presented a medical certificate from Dr Fellows-Smith.' They had reached the waiting-room downstairs. 'He's my doctor. National Health.'

'Mine too,' the archdeacon reflected with more interest. 'And National Health, naturally. Private care is well beyond my stipend.' Another thought struck him. 'What about the rice?' he asked, recalling for the first time in years a beating at school for flicking spoonfuls of soggy pudding across the dining-hall.

'I do not afford the food much thought.'

'I suppose you've got out of the diet, too?' the archdeacon asked sharply.

The chaplain tapped his midriff. 'The old duodenal ulcer.'

'What ulcer? Every time I dine at the palace, you scoff like a lumberjack.'

'These conditions recur. One is gripped, out of the blue. Inadequate diet could cause instant perforation of my ulcer, as a toe through an old sock. Undoubtedly fatal.'

'Another medical certificate, I suppose?'

The chaplain nodded vigorously. He stood on the windswept front step, rubbing his fat red hands. He had been wondering for months how to make an ally of Archdeacon Bellwether. Efficient, secretive, devious, the chaplain would have wormed his way through any organization which unwisely attached him to a powerful man. He could have felt equally fulfilled as adjutant to a regiment, Parliamentary private secretary, or some company chairman's personal assistant.

The weak old bishop had gratefully called the Revd Arthur Dawney his confidential clerk. He had left overlooked or undiscerned his ecclesiastical mischief. The strong new one had fair-mindedly acquiesced to keeping him, but every increase in effective episcopal power had reduced his chaplain's. Without an intrigue in hand, the Revd Arthur Dawney became as fretful as an old woman without her knitting.

'Such a splendid practice,' said the chaplain enthusiastically. Mr Bellwether agreed. The oldest and most respected medical partnership in the city was conducted in a well-mannered, quiet-spoken, unhurried way, which harmonized with its patients.

'I have a tendency to gout,' the archdeacon mentioned hopefully.

'Well, give it a try,' the chaplain encouraged him. 'The workpeople at the local factories get whole weeks off for imaginary illnesses.'

'My gout is *not* imaginary,' the archdeacon

told him brusquely.

'Of course not. Well, good morning, Bill. It's heart-warming to find the bishop home so full of energy, isn't it?'

The cathedral clock was striking the half-hour. At nine, the archdeacon had to chair the Parsonage Maintenance Committee. He recalled that Dr Fellows-Smith was renowned to be tetchy in the morning, but to mellow by lunch.

3

The blare of a horn and the screech of tyres shattered the archdeacon's sombre midday contemplation in the Old Chapterhouse Surgery forecourt. He jumped like the bishop once grasping for the ball during a line-out at Twickenham.

'Can't you look where you're going, instead of waddling about like a pregnant penguin?' came a cross female voice from a low, glossy, scarlet Ferrari. 'Why, it's the archdeacon. Good morning, Mr Bellwether,' said Mrs Elizabeth Arkdale, FRCOG.

The archdeacon raised a smile. 'He protects His own,' he murmured with a grateful glance skywards. 'Pray do not feel guilty.'

'Guilty? I'm not feeling in the slightest guilty. You stepped straight into my path. Why is a man like you, obviously busting at the gussets with robust health, visiting the doctor?'

The smile dissolved in a look of self-pity. 'My gout. I'm a martyr to it.'

'Gout? Congratulations. There's a cure.

Live on sixpence a day, and earn it. Prescribed by Mr Abernethy of Bart's in the last century, never bettered.' She slammed the car door. 'How's the bishop?'

'He wants us on morning runs, as if schoolboys.'

'What a super idea. It'll tune up your arteries like organ pipes.'

Liz Arkdale was a quick-moving squall through the blue skies of Mitrebury society. She was consultant gynaecologist and obstetrician at the Infirmary. She was slim and pretty, her hair the colour of newly-minted pennies, her legs undervalued by the anatomical function of simply moving her about, her personality as compelling of attention as an ambulance siren.

Nobody in Mitrebury had really grown used to Liz Arkdale. She knew all in the county who counted, from the Duke of Westshire to the manager of the handiest betting-shop. She could arrange anything from invitations to the bishop's garden-party to a plumber in an emergency on a Sunday. She claimed to be thirty-five, so that mean persons who looked her up in the public library's *Medical Directory*, discovered that she amazingly qualified as a doctor aged sixteen.

The waiting-room was empty save for Mr Windows.

'Oh! The medical madam. I'm all of a tizzy. The other two doctors say Dr Carmichael is ill, and he doesn't believe them.'

'Sensible man. Where are they?' She followed Mr Windows' finger into the sitting-room. The archdeacon was left again standing nervously on the doorstep.

'I was calling only to obtain an aegrotat,' he explained meekly to Mr Windows. 'Our new, active bishop, you know ... he is such an enthusiast for physical fitness.'

'What we call a health nut,' Mr Windows concurred gravely.

'Exactly. He desired the clergy to run about Mitrebury in luminous stripes and live on boiled rice, both of which I feel ruinous to my delicate constitution.'

'Oh, you're after what we of the medical profession call a "sick note"?'

'A dispensation,' Mr Bellwether agreed. 'The latin seemed more dignified.' He continued hopefully,

'As I *am* connected myself with the profession, by membership of the Health Service Family Practice Committee–'

'Take a pew,' Mr Windows invited. 'Though with poor Dr Carmichael suffering from what seems the hepatic liver, you might be in for a long wait.'

Inside the comfortable, threadbare sitting-room, all four doctors were staring at one another gloomily.

'One thing's for sure, Roland,' Liz Arkdale was apologizing, with a squeeze of his hand. 'You've got nothing that I can diagnose, being a gynaecologist.'

She sat on the arm of Roland's armchair, holding a tomato-juice. She wore a scarlet peasant blouse embroidered with gold, a black velvet skirt, black tights and gold-buckled shoes. 'I only called because ... well, I've just been examining a young married woman in my clinic, who was referred to the Infirmary by this practice. She complained to you that she'd "seen nothing" for six weeks. She was pregnant.'

'Well?' asked Freddie. 'What's wrong with that?'

'Only that you referred her to the eye clinic. Oh, you're darling doctors,' Liz said fondly. 'But you're as rusty as Florence Nightingale's lamp. I'm sure you've got a jar of leeches hidden somewhere, Freddie. Do you still advise delicate young women to wear cholera belts? Or perhaps chastity belts?' She raised from the worn carpet an ungainly piece of apparatus trailing wires. 'Do you *still* use this for deep heat treatment? I wouldn't use it to defrost a frozen turkey.'

'Our patients certainly don't seem to think we're past it,' Biggin told her stiffly. 'We've hardly time for our regular afternoon round of golf.'

'Of course, you've each got a bedside manner which would make a geriatric ward feel like a nursery school,' Liz agreed generously. 'But take it from me, medically you're doing Mitrebury as much good as a flu epidemic.'

'Why don't you take a holiday?' she suggested with a smile. 'Think of the good it would do your patients.'

The doctors did not take this amiss. All three had adored Liz for years.

'I've a confession,' said Biggin. 'For months, I've been intending to ground myself as a doctor, but I couldn't let you two down.'

Freddie Fellows-Smith slowly tapped the glass case of his stuffed pheasant. 'Do you remember Lady Beckenham? A patient of mine.'

'Yes,' said Liz. 'She died last week.'

'She should never have ridden a bicycle at

ninety three,' Freddie said reprovingly. 'She was a kindly old soul, with a touching faith in the medical profession, which clearly was not misplaced. At a chirpy eighty, she made her will. All to me. The entire fortune.' He looked apologetic. 'That I might pursue my pursuits – I've already ordered a pair of new guns from Purdey's. But I couldn't hang up my stethoscope, without seeming a cad to my partners.'

'All you need are replacements,' Liz pointed out.

'Might be difficult,' Biggin reflected. 'We must find doctors of dignity.'

'Oh, I know you think you're all dignified enough for the Queen's bedchamber,' Liz told him. 'Though if you ask me, you're just pompous.'

'Pompous?' Freddie disagreed. 'That's just the tone one gets into, from addressing clergymen with their clothes off.'

'The Church is so particular about its doctors,' Biggin persisted. 'Odd, when you'd think them all so impatient getting to Heaven.'

Roland Carmichael rose from the shabby armchair and took from the wall a framed photograph of a hospital group, in which the three doctors' bun-faced youthful selves might he detected, with patience.

'Our year at St Boniface's,' he reminisced. 'We heard that two of our fellow-students recently gave birth to a pair of young doctors.' His finger indicated on the old picture a thin, serious dark young man. 'That's "Loony" Liston.'

Freddie pointed out a beefy, fair one. 'And "Rubberduck" Drake.'

'*Theirs* are genes we could rely on,' Biggin concurred.

'If young Drake's like his father, he'll play a decent game of rugger and have a fine voice for bawdy songs.' Freddie nostalgically hummed a few bars from The *Ball of Kirriemuir*, of which Liz knew more of the inexhaustible verses than he did. 'And Liston ... well, a bit of a swot. Dark and weedy and inclined to be artistic. Reads books, you know.'

'Where *are* these pocket Hippocrates?' Liz asked.

'I've no idea.' Roland replaced the picture. 'Anyway, to slip them into our shoes is as impractical as slipping a private hospital into the back garden. We'd never get it past the bureaucrat wallahs of the National Health Service.'

'In my young days,' Freddie reflected,

41

'when the medical profession was conducted with the well-bred mateyness of a gentleman's club, you simply invited your prospective partner to dinner and gave him asparagus. You can tell a lot about a man from the way he handles asparagus,' he added darkly.

Liz fell silent. National Health Service regulations had no menace to her. The regional chairman had adored her for years, too. Tracing the two young medical men should hold no difficulty. The dean of St Boniface's medical school had adored her since they were students together.

'I might be able to assist with the case,' she suggested. 'I'm up in London tomorrow, examining in obstetrics. I'll look into St Boniface's. The quarters of champagne in the doctors' bar are anyway the best value for money in Town.'

They were interrupted by a loud knock. 'The reverend gent,' announced Mr Windows, 'is becoming unfortunate.'

'I must fly,' Liz declared. 'I'm operating at the Infirmary, and my anaesthetist is of a nervous disposition, who often jumps the gun.'

'Still busy, Mrs Arkdale,' the archdeacon observed with an ingratiating smile at the doorway, 'bringing joy to womankind by delivering their little bundles of love?'

'I seem to bring more joy, Mr Archdeacon, removing them at an early stage from the letter-box. Bye.'

'Well?' Freddie asked Mr Bellwether inhospitably. 'I want my lunch.'

'I wondered, Dr Fellows-Smith, if I might have an ... er, "sick note"? My gout–'

'Gout? You haven't had an attack of gout since Candlemas three years ago. Are you suborning me to perjure myself?'

'No, no,' exclaimed the archdeacon. 'But you gave one to the bishop's chaplain–'

'How dare you, sir. Inviting me to break my Hippocratic oath, by discussing one patient's secrets with another.'

'I do apologize,' the archdeacon said miserably. 'Perhaps a morning jog will be beneficial after all.'

'Exactly what I should prescribe myself. A liver like yours needs shaking regularly, like a cocktail.'

Biggin made for the door. 'Time's getting on. See you on the first tee as usual?'

Roland pulled himself slowly from his chair. 'Young Liston and young Drake,' he reflected. 'I wonder what their handicaps are?'

4

The London road ran arrow-straight into Mitrebury, a causeway across the green billows of countryside, lined in summer by a foam of cow-parsley.

It had brought the Roman legions from Wales by forced marches to rout Queen Boadicea. It had borne Duke William of Normandy's army from Hastings for the abject surrender of Winchester. It had been crushed under the boots of British recruits from Waterloo to Dunkirk. It was rolled along by Americans in their white-starred jeeps and trucks to D-Day. Lucky is England, to enjoy such an easygoing wedlock with its history.

Early the next morning, it was disturbed by Liz Arkdale in her scarlet Ferrari. She did not trifle with speed-limits. She had only one ambition. Not to become Dame Elizabeth Arkdale – which she decided was straightforward, if you sought to deliver the babies of rising young politicians. Hers was unachievable. She wanted to win the Monza

44

Grand Prix in Italy.

Liz Arkdale was often in London. She had students to examine, committees to sit on, lectures to give and to listen to. She would have glittered among the consultants who illuminated any of its famous and ancient teaching hospitals. In Harley Street, her private practice would have carried their gratitude back to every part of the world. She contented herself with staid, peaceable Mitrebury, which she loved – and sometimes hated, and was sometimes bored by, which she found worse.

Sensitive about the solemnity of examinations to the students, she wore an expensive green dress which emphatically avoided smartness, like those chosen by junior royalty for laying foundation stones. Her mind was already on her meeting that evening. She had telephoned the Dean of St Boniface's the previous day, immediately after her operating list at the Infirmary.

The doctors' bar at St Boniface's was beside the refectory, small, dark-panelled, hung with photographs of sporting teams whose glories were forgotten, and portraits of famous St Boniface's doctors who had joined their patients in Heaven or Hell. At six o'clock, fair-haired young Dr Drake and

45

dark-haired Dr Liston were nervously waiting.

'A dry sherry, please,' said Dr Drake.

'Vodka on the rocks,' ordered Dr Liston.

'My usual Buck's fizz, Albert,' Liz told the old man behind the bar. 'I suppose the dean relayed to you the situation in Mitrebury?'

Both doctors nodded. She continued, 'Mitrebury itself I can only describe as a narcotic nook. And the Old Chapterhouse Surgery as a medical Stonehenge. The senior doctor's a shooting man, though I sometimes wonder if he kills more people than wildlife.'

'We've developed a big worry,' said Dr Drake.

'If we know enough medicine for general practice,' Dr Liston explained.

'You've just finished your year's pre-registration jobs in hospital, haven't you? So you've legally unleashed upon the patients for better or for worse – or until, unfortunately, death do you part.' Liz sipped her champagne-and-orange-juice. 'Working in hospital, you're one of a white-coated army. General practice is guerrilla warfare. It needs personality and quick wits. From all the dean told me on the telephone, I'm sure you've got both.'

Dr Liston's dark eyelashes fluttered. 'Mrs

Arkdale – if *we* did go into general practice, is there one piece of good advice you could give us?'

'Certainly. The best and oldest. It's all right to put a patient to bed, but not to take. You're neither married – why not?'

Dr Drake sighed romantically. 'I *was* to have been last month. But dear Roddy emigrated to practise in California. He left behind his collection of paperbacks, his André Previn records, his cricket bat and me. We were redundant to his new life-style.'

Liz sympathized. 'I know you're a doctor first and a woman second. But every girl carries – like a Victorian locket – the picture of herself in white at the church door, on a lovely afternoon with everyone looking on admiringly. Don't you ever wear a bra?' she enquired of Dr Liston severely.

'Only for exams and at inquests.'

'One of your jobs will be medical officer to the Theological College. I suspect the students will go down like flies. I must rush.' She finished her drink. 'I'm expecting triplets. Nothing complicated. But the babies you expect to be difficult, pop out like corks from badly chilled champagne. Those you expect to be like shelling peas, end up with you feeling you're pulling your feet from riding-boots on a hot afternoon. I only wanted to inspect you, and suggest you came to Mitrebury on Friday to case the joint. There's a bar on the train. Oh! There's one thing in Mitrebury you must absolutely promise me to do.'

'Yes, Mrs Arkdale?' the pair asked eagerly.

'See the fan vaulting in the lady chapel. Thirteenth century. Fantastic.' She rose. 'By the way, did I mention it? The three doctors you're replacing think you're men.'

She left them in the ancient hospital courtyard, always busy with nurses in scarlet-lined capes and caps cocked like doves' tails, white-coated doctors hurrying importantly, lounging students and well-muffled patients in wheelchairs.

'What the hell are we going to do in a dump like Mitrebury?' Lucy Drake exclaimed. She was dressed with professional severity in powder-blue jacket and skirt. 'Us? Unmarried and highly desirable, invited to every hospital party.'

'Let's give it a try,' argued Fay Liston lightly. She wore jeans and a T-shirt printed with the St Boniface's crest – quarterings of leeches, an amputation saw, blistering glasses and an Elizabethan enema syringe. It drew attention in discos. 'After all, it's been handed to us on a plate.'

'What about that haematology research job you were up for?'

'With a hundred other candidates.'

'I suppose we must think of our careers,' Lucy said earnestly. She saw life as a beautifully landscaped motorway to the grave. Fay saw it as a kaleidoscope, which she enjoyed shaking whenever bored with the view.

'Careers? The discrimination against women in medical jobs is disgraceful. Quite as bad as the conspiracy between doctors of both sexes to pretend otherwise.'

'Perhaps dear Roddy will send for me?' Lucy suggested optimistically. She took affairs of the heart as seriously as cardiology. 'Haven't you ever been in love?'

'Love is highly unenjoyable for one of my anxious personality. I worry tremendously if I'm worthy of him, and vice versa. It makes me terribly neurotic.'

They had reached the decorative hospital fountain, which had quietly bubbled away while a hundred generations of Londoners were born and died round it.

'Male doctors say all female ones are neurotic,' Lucy complained, as they sat on the edge of the stone basin. 'But we work harder, and generally we're better at it.'

'That's because our work is so much part of ourselves, isn't it, darling? With men, when they're not actually doing it, they forget it.'

'Like sex,' said Lucy.

'Man's love is of man's life a thing apart, 'Tis a woman's whole existence. Lord Byron.'

'Fay, you are so well read,' Lucy told her admiringly. 'Where did he say that?'

'In the *Oxford Dictionary of Quotations.*'

'I didn't think the famous obs and gobs consultant from rural Mitrebury would look a bit like that,' Lucy reflected. 'I'd always imagined Liz Arkdale as a beetroot in a little round hat, with a tweed jacket and skirt and enclosure tickets for the races in the buttonhole.'

'The dean must have told her we were absolutely brilliant.'

'More likely, he told her about you going topless to the last hospital ball.'

'Oh, what did it matter? Tits are doctors' bread and butter. God!' She clasped her T-shirt. 'I've lost it. My rabbit's foot.'

'Sometimes I despair of you.' Lucy used her severe voice. 'A highly educated, scientific woman, and you rely on primitive superstition.'

'Ah! Here it is.' Fay kissed the charm. 'It got me through my finals, my A-levels and my driving test. A hundred per cent success rate. Which is more than you can say for any operation.'

'Doctors don't believe in fairies.'

'Not so long ago, they didn't believe in germs.' She kissed it again. 'You know as well as I do, half a doctor's art is witchcraft, and the other half is convincing yourself that it isn't. Here's to Mitrebury. I'm not doing anything on Friday, anyway.'

'But general practice,' said Lucy cautiously. 'At the patients' beck and call, twenty-four hours a day. All work and no fun.'

'Work can be fun. And fun can become increasingly hard work.'

'You're right. You know our trouble? We're rapidly becoming a pair of mature women.'

Liz was at Mitrebury station on Friday morning in her Ferrari.

'We're driving out for lunch on Dr Freddie Fellows-Smith's farm,' she greeted them. 'He spends far longer there than in the surgery. His more nervous patients imagine he's a farmer doing a little doctoring as a hobby. How are you on asparagus? I insisted that Freddie provided it, out of season from Fortnum's, at great expense.'

Liz accelerated on the main road. 'Avoid getting the melted butter into your external, auditory meatus. Nervous?'

'Terrified,' said Fay.

'Panic-stricken,' said Lucy.

Liz smiled, overtaking a pair of lorries. 'The old doctors are dears – if one of the worst medical disasters since the Black Death. When I explained their young successors had undergone a change of sex, they were a weeny bit upset. Outrageous, unthinkable and preposterous were the words I recall. Freddie was amazed they let female students into St Boniface's at all. He said it used to be all rugger, beer and the Masons.'

'Er ... Mrs Arkdale,' said Lucy timidly. 'There's a police car right behind us.'

'Yes, doctor. I can see it in my mirror.'

'Er ... Mrs Arkdale,' murmured Fay deferentially. 'Isn't this a forty mile limit?'

'And I'm doing sixty? Yes, doctor. It is.'

'Didn't you ... er ... ought to...' Lucy suggested.

'Every cop car in the country has my number. They think I'm rushing to some poor woman in childbirth.' Liz exchanged waves with the crew as the police car passed. 'Sweet are the uses of maternity,' she observed.

The three old doctors were waiting in the

low, beamed sitting-room of Freddie's farm-house, their backs to a wide stone fireplace with crackling logs. Liz saw instantly they were more nervous than the two young guests. She introduced them. She heard Biggin mutter to himself, 'Wizard!'

'How's old Rubberduck Drake?' Freddie asked Lucy. 'I mean your father,' he apologized hastily.

'Very well, thank you,' Lucy told him politely.

'Old Loony Liston's not so bad, either.' Fay smiled. 'Could I have a vodka on the rocks?' she enquired of Roland Carmichael, hovering with the sherry decanter.

He blinked, as if she had required an injection of heroin.

'We're delighted to welcome a young Liston and young Drake,' Freddie continued. 'But we didn't think they'd be wearing pink frilly knickers.'

'Oh, really, Freddie,' Liz told him scathingly. 'Nobody wears those these days, except very peculiar men.'

'I'm sure you'll understand,' said Roland awkwardly. 'This practice demands doctors of great skill and long experience.'

'With a wise old eye for diagnosis,' mumbled Freddie over his pink gin.

'The dean of St Boniface's assured me that Dr Drake and Dr Liston were among his most knowledgeable students,' Liz told him impatiently.

'Oh, you think you know absolutely everything when you pass out of medical school,' he returned. 'It took me years to find out that I really knew nothing. Thank Heavens, it took the patients a few years more.'

An objection struck Biggin. 'Where shall they mess?'

'What mess?' Liz demanded shortly. 'Live, you mean? In the Old Chapterhouse Surgery. Mr Windows can look after them. There's enough room to house the entire Medical Women's Federation.'

'Been empty for years,' he persisted querulously. 'Hardly fit for delicate females.'

'Females aren't delicate any more,' Liz told him in exasperation. 'There's a law against it.'

They were interrupted by Mr Windows in his white jacket, announcing with the dignity of a first-class steward breaking up the captain's cocktail party that luncheon was served.

5

Neither young doctor knew that she was sitting the most searching examination of her life. With growing approbation, Freddie noticed they neither fussily cut their asparagus into morsels, nor pronged it like frankfurters. In a sound, practical way – to be expected of doctors – they seized it with their fingers, and with surgical delicacy dangled it into their mouths. Their well-shaped chins stayed undefiled of the butter which Mr Windows poured from a silver cream-jug (emblazoned with the crest of the P & O Shipping Company – he claimed it fell off the back of a boat).

Freddie suddenly groaned loudly. All stared in alarm.

'Sorry, the thought's just come back to me,' he apologized. 'You must find me a dull host. I've a distressing duty waiting me this afternoon. Euthanasia, you know.' He brushed his eye with the hand holding his glass of *Château Latour.*

'You practise it often, Dr Fellows-Smith?'

enquired Lucy, exchanging a startled glance with Fay.

'Only in the direst circumstances.'

'I'm sure it's often for the best,' agreed Fay compliantly

'Sara was so good a mother,' Freddie continued mournfully. 'So delightful a personality.'

'What's the diagnosis?' Lucy enquired gently.

'The red stomach worm.' She looked puzzled.

'My favourite sow,' he explained.

'But there's a new anthelmintic which cures it,' Fay told him brightly.

'What? You know all about pigs?'

'Well, I know all about worms. It's part of the pathology course.'

'You see?' Liz pointed out encouragingly. 'They're as useful diagnostically as decoratively.'

The atmosphere round the table began to warm, largely because Mr Windows, experienced in tongue-tied first nights at sea round the captain's table, distributed the claret as busily as a midsummer bee pollinating the flowers.

'Come to think of it,' mused Biggin, 'the women doctors during the war weren't

WAAFs, but RAF lady officers. Very decent chaps they were in the mess, too.'

'Somehow, I always imagined that women doctors wore brogues, smoked pipes, and percussed a chest as if driving home rivets,' Roland admitted. His eyes fell on his old hospital crest across Fay's T-shirt. 'But you seem to be bursting with the right hormones, Dr Liston, if I may say so.'

'And if I may say so,' Mr Windows interrupted gravely, 'the Old Chapterhouse Surgery needs a woman's touch worse than the Seven Dwarfs.'

Roland had been silent all through the meal. Now he pushed aside his saddle of lamb. 'I could hardly bring myself here today, Freddie,' he apologized. 'I felt so under the weather. If only I knew what it was,' he complained helplessly.

'Might be all in the mind?' suggested Biggin.

'The young doctor's always persuading himself he's got every disease in the world,' Freddie philosophized towards his two guests. 'The old one is always persuading himself that he's got nothing.'

'How long have you been suffering from lead poisoning, Dr Carmichael?' Fay asked pleasantly.

Everyone stopped eating.

'Exactly,' said Lucy calmly. 'I noticed the blue line on your gums when you smiled.'

'Which is absolutely diagnostic of the condition,' Fay added.

'That *would* fit in with my symptoms,' declared Roland, looking quickly at his two colleagues.

Freddie stared at the young doctors unbelievingly. 'But you haven't swallowed any lead,' he told Roland. 'Even if patients swing enough of it in the surgery.'

'Of course I haven't–' Roland stopped. He glared fiercely at Freddie. 'Lead shot,' he hissed. 'All that game you've been feeding me on, since Charlotte left me. There's so much lead in it, I sometimes wonder if you hit the poor beasts with an anti-tank gun.'

'But don't you eat with your glasses on, doctor?' Fay asked sweetly.

'Glasses? I don't need to wear glasses.'

'Oh, doctor!' said Lucy.

'I say,' exclaimed Biggin. 'It's just struck me, these two young ladies are exactly the replacements we need.'

'I was wondering how long you'd take to see the overwhelmingly obvious,' said Liz. 'Even without glasses, Dr Carmichael. Good. That's settled.'

'But the National Health Service rules and regulations–' started Biggin.

'The snag's Mr Bellwether,' Liz declared. 'Freddie, this claret is excellent. Where did you get it?'

'Sir George Prewitt's piles. For that relief, he expressed much thanks.'

'I happened to run into the archdeacon this morning,' Liz resumed. 'He was at the traffic lights, but only slightly grazed. The new doctors must come before the Family Practice Committee, where he's the chairman. He'll he dead against them, unless you give him a sick note to escape the bishop's cranky Hindu diet for lent.'

'Never! I will not perjure myself for one lead-swinger more experienced than the pendulum of Big Ben.'

Liz sighed. 'Life would be so much easier if the archdeacon succumbed to temptation by a steak-and-kidney pudding.'

The half-dozen doctors drove to the Old Chapterhouse Surgery. Lucy and Fay blinked at the salmon, the stag's head, the pews, the Farmers' Union calendar. 'We try to encourage a club like atmosphere,' Freddie explained affably. 'All those ghastly white walls and strip-lights in hospital. Enough to make you feel stretched out dead already.'

'You really should meet Archdeacon Bellwether,' said Liz thoughtfully, driving Lucy and Fay afterwards from the surgery forecourt to the station.

'Look out!' Lucy screamed.

A zebra crossing ran from the surgery to the cathedral. In its middle stood a large, dark-moustached, red-faced, Homburg-hatted man in clerical clothes, arms outstretched, mouth open, staring in horror. There was a bump. He disappeared.

'The archdeacon,' Liz exclaimed breathlessly. 'I've done it again. Third time since Monday.'

He was sitting on the crossing, staring blankly, gripping his left calf. Liz crouched, arms round him tenderly. 'My dear, dear Mr Bellwether! But you were rather behaving as though leading the Israelites across the Red Sea.'

'Where am I? Why, it's Mrs Arkdale. How terribly good of you to come and attend me so promptly,' he said bemusedly.

'You're in luck,' she told him. 'You've been run over by a car containing three doctors.'

He raised his eyes to Fay and Lucy. *Female* doctors?' he muttered. 'In Mitrebury? What about the Theological College?' he exclaimed. 'I was just conducting them

60

round the cathedral.'

Liz became aware that the inevitable crowd was composed of youthful clergymen.

'A couple of them can carry you into the surgery,' she ordered. 'It's always best on these occasions to escape before the police arrive and complicate everything.' She added to Lucy and Fay, 'You handle the case. For me, it's the wrong sex, and the wrong bit.'

The three old doctors were still talking to Mr Windows in the waiting-room.

'Scramble!' exclaimed Biggin urgently, as the archdeacon was carried in. 'Freddie – resuscitation!'

Freddie opened the resuscitation box. 'Damn! Only the bottle of port I was saving for my birthday.'

'I suppose you've got a tourniquet?' demanded Liz. 'He is bleeding quite a bit from his popliteal fossa.'

'We *had* one,' murmured Roland.

'We used it when the boiler leaked, doctor,' Mr Windows informed him.

'Well, a strong bandage,' Liz said impatiently. The archdeacon was laid on a pew, eyes shut, groaning loudly. 'Apart from anything else, the blood is quite ruining his trousers.'

'Dear me.' Biggin upturned an empty bin marked DRESSINGS. 'I *did* mean to order our surgical supplies last week.'

'Well, tie *something* round it.' Liz directed Lucy and Fay. 'Why isn't he wearing a tie?'

Lucy had slipped from her powder-blue jacket. She ripped off her white blouse, which she bound tightly round the patient's thigh.

'I say!' Biggin exclaimed, blinking at her. 'Reminds me of the old Mae West we used to wear.'

'Another bandage.' Lucy looked hard at Fay.

'But I've got no bra—'

'This is no time for modesty.'

Fay slipped off her T-shirt.

The archdeacon opened his eyes, and fainted. 'Shall I prescribe a dose of the medical comforts, doctor?' Mr Windows enquired discreetly of Freddie.

'Brandy, you mean? All round, I think. My best *Grande Champagne* from the bookcase. Except for the patient, of course. He can do with *sal volatile*.'

6

Liz next met Mr Bellwether three weeks later. It was shortly before Easter. She had slammed her Ferrari to a halt on a double yellow line outside Mitrebury City Hall, narrowly missing him on a tricycle.

'The bishop insists we renounce the motor-car,' he explained dolefully. 'And I never learned to ride the two-wheeled variety. I tried my niece's fairy-cycle, but I did so keep falling off.'

'How's the memento of our last little encounter?' she asked cautiously, slamming the car door.

'Healed perfectly, I'm glad to say. It looked much worse than it was.'

'How fortunate you had those two clever and dedicated young doctors to succour you.'

'Yes,' said the archdeacon dully.

'Still taking the bishop's diet?'

He nodded miserably. 'I feel extremely poorly on it. I get no sympathy from Dr Fellows-Smith. He says I must have a tapeworm, like his dog.'

'Lady doctors will be much easier over sick notes than hard-hearted male ones,' she continued coaxingly.

The archdeacon looked stern. 'Mrs Arkdale, you oblige me to tell you that I do not believe that women should ever become priests, or policemen or physicians. Or prime ministers.'

'Only pregnant, I suppose?'

'They're unsuited to Mitrebury,' he said lamely. 'Remember the fuss over the lady traffic wardens? And where are you off to?'

'The races. But first the Family Practice Committee. To interview the two successors for the Old Chapterhouse Surgery.'

The archdeacon frowned. 'But Mrs Arkdale, you're not on it.'

'Nonsense! I'm on every National Health committee in Mitrebury.'

She preceded him into the City Hall.

They were directed to a bleak, chilly room with a long, baize-covered paper-strewn table. Mr Bellwether took the centre chair. 'Many apologies for absence,' he murmured, picking up a wad of letters. 'The races, I suppose?'

'Please be through by 3.30.' Liz sat with three other committee members. 'I happen to know the winner.'

All the local racehorse owners adored her, too.

'Mrs Arkdale, are you sure–'

'My dear man, you *are* being tedious. Of course I'm on this committee. But as I must declare a personal interest in the two candidates, I shall keep my mouth firmly shut during the entire proceedings.'

'Lady doctors?' muttered the retired colonel on her right. 'Could create problems, you know. I haven't taken my clothes off in front of a strange woman since I liberated Brussels.'

The pair were summoned. Lucy wore navy blue. Fay had a long cotton skirt and a batik blouse, her dark hair in a crimson velvet headband. They sat demurely on a pair of hard chairs. Their first questioner was a fat man in an expensive suit, inviting their views on the pharmaceutical industry.

'As you own that drug factory which sprawls across the countryside and completely spoils the view,' Liz told him. 'Your question's as loaded as a poacher's pocket.'

'Mrs Arkdale!' protested the archdeacon.

'Oh, just ignore me. Pretend I'm not here.' She shut her mouth firmly, folded her arms and glared at him.

'Where would doctors be without your research?' Fay answered wisely. 'We name it, you cure it.'

'May I disagree?' Lucy was always forthright. 'You spend millions of pounds every year, advertising drugs which the doctors don't understand and the patients don't need.'

'That's my girl!' exclaimed a bald, lanky man, the Labour candidate for Mitrebury. 'They should have been nationalized years ago.'

'Do shut up, Ron,' requested Liz. 'We're here to appoint a couple of doctors, not hold a conference on the nation's economy.'

Mr Bellwether turned indignantly. 'Mrs Arkdale! You are no more here than the Archangel Gabriel.'

'I'm speaking for him. What Mitrebury needs is a super pair of female doctors. And there they are.'

'I shall start asking *sensible* questions,' the archdeacon said forcefully. 'Dr Liston, what branch of medical science are you most interested in?'

'The nervous system.'

'Oh, really?' he broke off. 'Perhaps *you* could explain something sorely troubling me since Mrs Arkdale nearly murdered – er, my unfortunate accident. Why these tingling sensations up my arms? Why do I feel I was walking in diving boots? Dr Fellows-Smith is baffled. He tells me that if I was a horse I'd have the staggers.'

Fay's mind had the quickness of a flash-bulb. She remembered the conversation at lunch in the farmhouse. 'I suppose you're taking a normal diet?'

'I most certainly am not! For most of Lent I've been compelled by our bishop – a splendid man, if inclined to over-emphasize that all flesh is but grass,' he added hastily, 'to exist on rice and water. Plus sips of milk – goat's being unobtainable from Unigate.'

'What sort of rice?' Lucy asked. The committee stared fascinated.

'Just rice,' he replied helplessly. 'My wife buys it from the supermarket.'

'I'm afraid you're suffering from beri-beri,' Fay announced.

'Great heavens!' He leapt up, scattering his papers. 'How horrid! Is it catching? Oh, dear me! Shall I be shunned, like the leper in Leviticus?'

'You *have* got a flair for diagnosis,' Liz exclaimed to Fay admiringly. 'You usually get beri-beri in places like Kampuchea – it's a vitamin deficiency. Treatment, doctors, please?' she demanded in her exam-room voice.

'Just a good mixed diet,' said Fay. 'And certainly no exertion.'

'Correct. I now propose we appoint these two brilliant doctors. Seconded, Ron? Passed unanimously. I'm taking you down to the Infirmary, Mr Bellwether. My colleagues on the medical wards will be enormously interested in a tropical disease of malnutrition occurring in an English cathedral town.'

'Shall you write it up for the *Lancet?*' Lucy asked excitedly.

'*Lancet* hell. This goes into the *Guinness Book of Records*. Come to the races? I've arranged the Dom Pérignon to be already on ice.'

7

'How did you sleep?' asked Lucy.

'As well as anyone could in Fingal's Cave,' said Fay.

It was a month later, St Philip and St James's Day. The pale spring sun was warming for the six hundredth-odd time the stone of the cathedral spire – a soaring icicle on the clear, cold nights, when the furrowed black countryside sparked in morning frosts and trapped lagoons of mist.

The two young doctors had come down to breakfast, their first morning in the Old Chapterhouse Surgery. The sitting-room table had a shining cloth and glittering silver, its crests representing famous shipping lines which once strung together the British Empire. Mr Windows wore a fresh white coat, napkin neatly folded over forearm.

'A slice of Sara, doctors?' invited Mr Windows, napkin folded over forearm. They stared at him. 'Ham,' he explained, serving from the silver salver. 'Dr Fellows-Smith's sow succumbed in the end, poor animal. He

69

ran over her in error with his tractor. Life is strange. Did you mention Fingal's Cave, doctor?' Fay nodded. 'That's strange, too. It was her favourite piece of music.'

'Whose?' Fay asked, as he hummed a few bars.

'Dr Fellows-Smith's Aunt Clara. No wonder your apartments upstairs are a shade damp. They haven't been aired since she died in them.'

'What of?' Lucy was fascinated.

'Something lingering, doctors. I fancy it was the renal kidneys.'

'I'm suffering acute doubts,' Lucy said as he left them. She wore a snuff-coloured skirted jersey suit, having pondered as deeply on the sartorial as clinical demands of Mitrebury.

'Why? We can try it a few months.' Fay had a bright Indian skirt, a plain blouse and her headband. 'It could be exciting fun living here. Compared with an Outer Hebrides bird sanctuary.'

'Only six months ago,' Lucy said tragically. 'I thought I was going to enjoy a loving marriage, a fulfilling career, intellectual companionship and genetically satisfying motherhood.'

'I never understood why Roddy fancied

you.' Fay was not sympathetic at breakfast.

'Oh you're always so businesslike about your men.'

'I'm businesslike about dining out, going to the theatre, taking holidays. Why not my other enjoyments? Did I ever tell you that dear Roddy once tried to make me?'

'No!'

'It was when we were doing casualty together.'

'What happened?' Lucy asked nervously.

'We were too busy. You know what casualty's like.'

'Perhaps Roddy *was* rather thick,' Lucy admitted. 'He'd never have passed his finals, if I hadn't coached him in bed. His respiration was dreadfully weak and his metabolism practically non-existent. We *did* have a lot of rows, I suppose,' she reflected fondly.

'Naturally. You're the argumentative type.'

'I'm not!'

'Yes, you are.'

'I most certainly am *not*.'

'Everyone at St Boniface's called your dear Roddy "the stalactite".'

Lucy looked puzzled. 'Why?'

'Because he was a monumental drip.'

The sound of organ music burst from the waiting room. They stared at each other.

'Do you suppose we're MO's to the cathedral choir?' Lucy asked anxiously. 'I know absolutely nothing about the larynx.'

Mr Windows had opened a portable ship's harmonium at the bottom of the stairs, and was singing *Abide With Me*.

'...*Change and decay, in all around I see,* a little present from the late doctors,' he broke off. 'For my services to humanity.'

'Mr Windows,' asked Lucy firmly. 'Exactly how much medicine do you know?'

'Doctor's steward afloat taught me a lot about our mutual profession. Everything from boils to bubonic,' he imparted with dignity. 'As for handling emergencies, I remember one Christmas Day off Hong Kong, when a Chinese steward went berserk with the carver during dinner. Sliced a passenger's ear off. Fell into the captain's soup. Mind, you had to laugh.'

'Look at this, Mr Windows.' Unimpressed with the reminiscences, Lucy displayed dust which the stair-rail had transferred to her palm.

'And that stag's head must be as insanitary as an alley-cat,' Fay complained.

'No harm in old Tiberius,' Mr Windows flicked it with a feather duster. 'He's been dead and stuffed for twenty years. Some of the patients remember their mothers keeping their minds off tonsils and measles with him. Now they themselves is coming up with the rheumatics and bronchitics, and others of what we in the medical profession call the disintegrative diseases. Old Tiberius just hung there inscrutable, what you might call a horned sphinx. If only he could speak, he'd be an encyclopaedia of medical information, better than any professor. As well as knowing a few choice details about a lot of people in Mitrebury.'

There was a loud cracked clang. The doctors jumped.

'The doorbell,' Mr Windows explained, instantly sticking his duster back in the umbrella stand.

'Our first patient,' Lucy said quietly.

'Good luck, Lucy.'

'Good luck, Fay.'

They exchanged glances – excited, scared, proud, sentimental, amused, all at once. Impulsively, they clasped each other.

'I'm delighted to see you're so fond,' said Liz Arkdale dryly from the door. 'I looked in to wish you luck. Though heaven knows, the patients need that, not the doctors. Any worries?'

'Yes,' said Fay at once. 'We said at St

73

Boniface's we didn't think we knew enough medicine. Now we're sure of it.'

'A very good general practitioner need know very little medicine,' Liz comforted them. 'Take the typical consultation – one person reasonably fit, the other stressed, overweight, full of bad habits, lacking exercise and sleep. That's the doctor. Most people won't come to you because they're sick. Only to be reassured they're not. Others will be old, or disabled, wanting your help soldiering on to the end of the battle of life. Some can't cope with the emotions of others – or with their own. The rest of the diseases will be those featured on TV the night before.' She picked a strange metal instrument from the desk. 'What *did* the old doctors use *this* for?' she asked, mystified.

'Dr Fellows-Smith crushed up the bones, madam,' Mr Windows told her.

Liz dropped it. 'Ugh!'

'It was his duck press.' Mr Windows took it with an offended look.

'I suppose you've a lot to live up to,' Liz admitted. 'The three old doctors may have been as dangerous as a toadstool in a basket of mushrooms, but they were mentioned more often in Mitrebury than the Father, Son and Holy Ghost.'

'Any more advice?' Lucy asked.

Liz considered, 'Yes. Remember the middle-class woman has two spouses. Her husband and her weight. She fusses over and closely watches both, and responds equally to the benevolence or unkindness of either.' She pulled down Lucy's lower eyelid. 'I don't much care for that.'

'Surely I'm not anaemic?' Lucy exclaimed.

'Too much eye-liner. And if you persist in going topless under your blouse, Dr Liston, you're going to have the heaviest medical work-load in Mitrebury.'

'What else is there but work, Mrs Arkdale?' Fay suggested archly. 'I'm afraid Mitrebury's going to be dull after living in hospital with a lot of men.'

'Do you imagine *I* didn't find the same?' Liz told her. 'How insulting.'

'But you've got a husband,' said Lucy.

'Yes, and I've had him a long time,' she complained. 'Now I've got an urgent case at Fenny Bottom.'

'Still busy bringing the world twinkling little babies, madam?' enquired Mr Windows, opening the front door.

'Mr Windows, by now you should know that babies do not twinkle. They are pink and noisy and unreliable in their habits at both ends. Must fly.'

The door shut. The bell rang. The two young doctors stared at each other again.

'This *must* be our first patient,' declared Lucy.

Fay was searching in her blouse. 'I've lost it!'

'Not your stethoscope?'

'My rabbit's foot. Ah–!' Fay kissed it. The door opened for a man in a green overall, with a bright red nose and clasping an armful of bottles.

'The weekly drinks order,' he announced cheerfully. 'I trust the new doctors will be continuing their valued custom?'

'That's enough to open a pub,' Lucy exclaimed in horror. 'We most certainly are not.'

'The late doctors did enjoy their home comforts,' Mr Windows enlightened her.

'Morning, Mr Shelburne,' he greeted a dark-suited man in the doorway.

'Have I the honour of addressing the inheritors of the practice?' Mr Shelburne smiled. 'I call to reassure you that *should* anything go wrong, I am always available.' Lucy looked puzzled, as he handed her a card. 'We are the longest established of

Mitrebury's undertakers. By a happy co-incidence, we started the same year as this practice, with which we have always enjoyed a most congenial relationship. We like to think that we look after your patients, doctor, with the same care as you do.'

'At least, you know they're not malingering,' Fay told him tartly.

'Our charges are *most* competitive, as we always have our eye on the overheads,' he assured them, solemnly looking heavenwards. 'As I *am* here, doctor–' He pushed up his sleeve. 'Perhaps you'd have a look at my dermatitis? Dr Hill thought it was occupational.'

'Could you do anything about my red nose?' the delivery man asked Fay, while Mr Windows stowed the bottles in the resuscitation box. 'It fair baffled the last doctors. It's embarrassing, as I hardly touch a drop.'

'I can't do *anything* in the middle of the waiting-room,' she told him.

'Does it itch?' the delivery man asked Mr Shelburne curiously. 'My nose sort of glows, you know. On a cold morning, the wife says she can warm her hands on it.'

'Please sit down, both of you,' Lucy directed hastily. The telephone rang.

8

'Hello?' said Lucy into the telephone. 'This *is* the doctor. Your toddler's stuck *where* and screaming his head off? That's a job for the fire brigade, not the medical profession. Haven't you got a saw? Not that sort of sore,' she continued impatiently. 'I mean a sawing saw.'

She turned from the telephone to find the waiting room swept by the incoming tide of patients, with their children, prams, shopping-baskets and dogs.

'Funny, what people ring up the doctor about,' Mr Windows reflected. 'You wouldn't believe what, last week a woman had got stuck up her vacuum cleaner. Never thought to switch the current off. You had to laugh.'

'Come along, sit down on the pews,' Lucy directed nervously, 'Who's first?'

'I am,' everyone shouted.

The telephone rang.

Fay answered it. 'This is the *new* doctor. Gran's took queer again? Only different? But how can I know how she's took queer

78

this time if I didn't know how she was took queer last time? She was took queer *then* the same as she was took queer at Christmas? But I wasn't here at Christmas, was I? *Now* she's took queer like she was took queer in Benidorm? And I wasn't there, either. Where do you live? I'll call.' The telephone rang again as she jotted down the address. 'You answer it,' she commanded Mr Windows.

'Haven't we an appointment system?' Lucy asked him desperately.

'No, the late doctors just sat 'em down. First bum, first served.' He continued into the telephone. 'The two-thirty at Sandown? The second favourite? Right, I've got that–'

'Where are the patients' records, Mr Windows?' Fay demanded frantically.

'Records? No, the late doctors weren't great scribblers. They had such good memories. The first race at Newmarket?' he resumed. 'Pip-Pip, a dead cert–'

'You mean, there's not a single note on any patient?' Lucy asked in panic.

'Come to think of it, doctor, there were some notes in Dr Hill's old RAF tin trunk.'

'Then where is it?'

'Lost months ago. I think it got mixed with Aunt Clara's effects.'

'What's that phone call?' Lucy added angrily.

'The practice racing tipster. Calls every morning. Most reliable. Makes us quite a pile.'

Lucy snatched the telephone. 'The service is discontinued. Mother!' she snapped, putting it down. 'Will you please stop your little boy from kicking to bits this rather nice antique desk?'

'Found the records, doctor!' Mr Windows triumphantly held up a leather-bound ledger.

Fay opened it. 'October the first,' she read out. 'Shot a brace of pheasant and catheterized a rector's prostate.' She stared at the cover. *'Game and Fishing Book?'*

'Dr Fellows-Smith took a sporty view of his profession,' Mr Windows explained.

Fay banged down the book. 'Mr Windows! You are about as much use in this practice as a midwife in a nunnery.'

He drew himself up. 'Indeed, doctor? I have been a feature of the Old Chapterhouse Surgery longer than old Tiberius,' he said with the chill, majestic menace of an iceberg. 'Now what happens? Sacking the racing tipster. Stopping the drinks order. Wanting records what we ain't got. Appointments! I ask you. As though we was a poncy hairdresser's. Everything changed! You might as well take the choir stalls out of the cathedral and put in them cocktail stools. It's sacrilege. I'm abandoning ship.'

He pushed through the crowd of patients and stamped upstairs.

Lucy was appalled. 'We can't do without Mr Windows.'

'Why not?' demanded Fay.

'The last doctors thought the world of him.'

'Oh, yes. If he'd died, they'd have had him stuffed and put in a glass case, too.'

'Who'll do the cooking?'

'We will.'

'Nonsense. We're both experts on vitamins and healthy diets, and neither of us can boil an egg. Besides,' she added compassion- ately, 'where's the poor man going?'

'Back to his old job of picking ears from the captain's soup.'

'Be serious!'

'I am being serious.'

'You're not in the slightest.'

'There you go, Lucy, arguing as usual.'

'I am *not* arguing.'

Fay was aware of a sharp pain in her right knee. 'You kick me again,' she said, spinning round to glare at the little boy, 'and I'll give you such a smack bottom you'll be watching telly standing for a week.'

Lucy decided firmly, 'We're going to crawl to Mr Windows'

'Tapeworm,' said Fay.

He was descending the stairs, seaman's kitbag on his shoulder. 'I shall send for my things tomorrow,' he informed them, with the air of Captain Bligh set adrift from the *Bounty*. 'Please see they take great care over my harmonium.'

Each taking an arm, the two doctors hustled him into the sitting-room.

'Can't we entice you aboard again?' Lucy demanded desperately.

'Who wants patients' records?' asked Fay lightly. 'The last doctors probably got all the diagnoses wrong, anyway.' She slipped an arm round his neck. 'You're not going to leave two weak little women alone in this big, tough practice, are you?'

'I have resisted female wiles all the way from Tynemouth to Tokyo,' he told her severely. 'And from Swansea to Santiago.'

'Why, you've got a lump on your neck,' Fay exclaimed.

'That's my barnacle,' he told her casually.

Interested, Lucy took it between her fingers. 'It's a lipoma.'

'Or a sebaceous cyst?' Fay frowned.

Mr Windows looked alarmed. 'Nothing serious, I hope, doctor?'

Lucy's eye caught Fay's. 'Well, it could *turn* nasty.'

'I should advise you to keep it under constant medical supervision,' Fay added.

'I always knew I had a dermal skin,' he admitted uneasily. He hesitated. 'And I think I've got a gastric stomach, doctor. For years now, I've suffered a sort of landlocked sea-sickness.'

'But why didn't you consult the other doctors?' Lucy asked, puzzled.

'That lot?' he asked scornfully. 'Not on your Nelly. I never trusted them. They were too disorganized.'

'Will you trust us?' Lucy asked in a humble voice. 'Even if we're women?'

Mr Windows gave a slow smile. 'Don't mind me, doctor. I resigns about once a week. It's the only way a bloke can get himself appreciated.' He jerked his head towards the waiting-room. 'Want me to sort that lot out?'

Mr Windows threw open the door. 'Right! Who's on the red medicine?' he demanded fiercely. 'Port side, over here. Who's on the green? Starboard, over there. Who's after a day off? Sick notes under the stag.'

The patients gathered obediently in silent groups. 'Shall I play them something cheerful on my harmonium, doctor?' Mr Windows offered benignly. 'It does so help them to pass the time.'

The two doctors started work to *All Things Bright and Beautiful.* Some of the patients joined in. It seemed that Mr Windows' performances were as much an attraction at the Old Chapterhouse Surgery as Reg Dixon once was at the Tower Ballroom, Blackpool.

'But Mr Hargreaves!' Lucy exclaimed to the middle-aged engineer facing her across the desk of her cramped consulting-room. 'How *long* have you been taking this medicine of yours?'

'Fifteen years, two months and four days, doctor.'

Lucy frowned. 'Is it doing you any good?'

'Well, it's not doing me any harm.'

'Do you know why Dr Hill prescribed it for you?' she asked, more puzzled.

'Can't say, doctor. I used to come in, and Dr Hill would say, "I suppose you want some more of your medicine?" He was such a nice gentleman, I didn't want to upset him. So I said yes. For fifteen years, two months and four days.'

'But I don't think there's anything the slightest wrong with you.'

'Neither do I, doctor. For the last five years I haven't been taking it. As I didn't care to throw it away, I've been stacking the bottles in the garage. I can hardly get the Mini in. But it kept Dr Hill happy, didn't it?'

In the consulting-room next door, Fay was reassuring the mother of the boy who had kicked her. 'I honestly don't think you should worry that he's delicate. It's when children *don't* kick things, when they sit about and mope, then's the time to get worried.'

'That's a real relief, I must admit. Dr Fellows-Smith said if his beagle behaved like that, he'd have him put down.'

Fay smiled, opening the consulting-room door. 'Dr Fellows-Smith only confuses humans with animals because he loves both so much.'

Freddie himself was standing in the front door. With his back to him, Lucy's patient was enthusiastically telling the waiting crowd, 'The new lady doctor's a real wonder. The old 'uns weren't a patch on her.'

'Good morning, Dr Fellows-Smith,' Fay

85

said loudly.

'Mum,' demanded the little boy shrilly. 'Can I kiss the doctor?'

'He never wanted to kiss *me*,' said Freddie gruffly. 'I looked in in case you needed any help. It seems to me, I'll be most use to the practice if I go back to my golf.'

9

'Why, it's the archdeacon,' said the bishop. 'Good evening, Bill. Keeping well, I hope?'

It was Ascension Day, a fortnight later. The swallows and the tourists had returned to Mitrebury. The bishop was strolling with his chaplain through the warm twilight from the cathedral to his palace.

Mr Bellwether gripped his waistcoat. 'I wish I could say as much. But I suffer the most terrible stomach ache. Since Lent,' he added pointedly.

'No one was sorrier at your indisposition than I,' the bishop told him easily. 'But I fancy it was much your own fault, Bill, for not taking vitamin pills like the rest of us. And Dr Fellows-Smith was *most* generous with your sick-leave. I hope you'll soon be joining our morning fun again?'

Mr Bellwether gripped his leg. 'I have far from recovered after my motor-accident. At my age, the body needs time to repair itself. The skeleton becomes brittle, I believe, like well-roasted crackling.'

'But my dear Bill! I saw you running yesterday as though you had your eye on an Olympic gold medal, not a Mitrebury bus.'

'It comes and goes,' said the archdeacon hastily.

'You can't leave the jogging to the Theological College and myself.' The bishop became more commanding than consoling. 'To share a burden is a gift in itself, Bill.'

'I shall consult Dr Liston about my state of health, Peter,' he promised sulkily.

'Let us earnestly hope that she can pass you as fighting fit. Our young lady doctors seem to be making an excellent impression in Mitrebury,' the bishop continued to his chaplain, as Mr Bellwether walked away with a pronounced limp.

'They do not even dress professionally,' the Revd Arthur Dawney objected severely. 'The dark one has orange trousers.'

'Surely medical ladies have outgrown the button-boot and blue stocking image?' The bishop was amused. 'Personally, I find nothing more unfeminine than a feminist.'

'I dined at the Theological College last night.' They continued their stroll. 'The principal was gravely concerned over his official doctors.'

'Why not? They have their heads screwed

on the right way.'

'They have everything screwed on the right way, if I may be vulgar,' the chaplain said forcefully. 'There is an epidemic of minor illness among the students.'

'And a good thing too,' returned the bishop. 'It will counteract the bad publicity of "gay priests". Though if you ask me, Arthur, that sort of thing would be eliminated by the younger clergy taking regular and vigorous exercise.'

'When Dr Fellows-Smith was the college doctor, he advocated for such persons a brisk hosing-down in the stable-yard.'

'The new doctors are most useful to my Teenage Mothers' Group. A lady clearly prefers to consult one of her own sex on conditions which they share, just as you and I might he reluctant to on conditions which we do not.'

'I was brought up to remove nothing but my hat in the presence of a lady.'

The bishop thought it best to change the subject. 'Did you know that next month our new young Duchess of Westshire will be producing her first child?'

'Some matters are not beyond my powers of observation.'

'A christening!' The bishop rubbed his

large hands, 'The Duchess is a great favour-ite with the newspapers. I was planning to install the TV crew in the nave, so the cameras could get the Duchess and myself in two-shot at the font. Why so shocked?' he asked with raised eyebrows.

'The last bishop even frowned upon the *Mitrebury Echo*.'

'The last bishop – may his soul rest in peace – had no notion about influencing important opinion. No more than perform-ing our yearly stint, reading the prayers for a fortnight in the House of Commons. And one can make such excellent contacts *there,*' he murmured, 'if one is not so narrow-minded to avoid the strangers' bar. We must move with the times, Arthur. We are no longer Christian soldiers, but God's public relations officers. It costs a hundred and fifty million a year to run the Church. And not one penny in advertising budget! So we must develop our in-house publicity.'

He held up his pectoral cross in the lamplight. 'Not a hard sell, surely? Have we not the greatest logo in the world? By the way, I think I'm getting ITV interested in screening the daily life of the dean and chapter as an ongoing series, but they're being rather sticky over the residuals.'

They had reached the steps of the palace. 'Are you yourself remaining with the Old Chapterhouse practice?' asked the chaplain.

'Yes, though my doctor is immaterial, as I am never ill,' said the bishop with satisfaction.

The Revd Arthur Dawney recognized – as Lambeth Palace and Downing Street recognized with a smile – that the Bishop of Mitrebury had his eye on an archbishopric, as keenly as once upon the goalposts of Twickenham and the Australian bowling. The soundest qualification for the job was outliving all rivals.

'You're dining with the chief constable tonight, Peter?'

'No, it had to he postponed. Mr McTavish is taking the chair at a valedictory dinner to Drs Carmichael, Hill and Fellows-Smith in the Bishop's Arms. A well-deserved tribute, I'm sure. The three must have brought many Mitrebury citizens into the world.'

'And pushed many more out of it,' said the chaplain under his breath.

It was a tribute which occasioned Roland Carmichael and Freddie Fellows-Smith to be arm-in-arm in Mitrebury High Street at midnight, wearing dinner-jackets and singing,

'*Caviar comes from the virgin sturgeon, Virgin sturgeon, very fine fish. Virgin sturgeon needs no urgin', That's why caviar's a very rare dish.*'

'Taxi!' yelled Roland across the empty roadway.

'*My father was the keeper of the Eddystone Lighthouse,*' Freddie continued raucously. '*He saw a mermaid out at sea. The result of his sins were a couple of twins, The first was caviar the other was me.*'

'Why aren't there any taxis about?' Roland complained irately. 'The drivers are all scrimshanking, like half our patients.'

Freddie stopped on the pavement. 'Isn't that old Biggin's vintage Bentley?'

Roland squinted. 'So it is. Outside the police station.'

'Damn silly place to park.'

'He'll give us a lift. Come on.' They hooked their arms round each other's shoulders.

'*I gave caviar to my girl-friend,*' they shouted. '*She was a virgin staunch and true, I gave caviar to my girl-friend, Now there's nothing she won't do.*'

'Hey, Biggin!' Roland yelled. He turned to Freddie, blinking. 'He's gone into the police station. With a policeman.'

'Let's go in, too,' Freddie suggested heartily.

92

Inside the police-station, Biggin Hill was observing, 'So you're in the police force, Timothy Wilkins? Well, fancy that. I thought you were still at school.'

The police-station lobby was square, with a counter and a pair of wooden benches as hefty as park seats. Its mustard-painted walls were decorated only with posters warning about the dangers of muggers and the Colorado beetle. The chief constable of Mitrebury believed in police stations being as unpleasant as possible, to discourage the public from being obliged to use them.

Its other occupant was fair-haired, fresh-faced PC Wilkins.

'You *were* asleep at the wheel of your car, doctor,' said PC Wilkins seriously. 'That's why I had to ask you to step inside.'

'Awfully kind of you, Timothy. I've had a very long day, and a very long dinner. I should simply love a cup of coffee.' He yawned deeply.

'It's not quite that, doctor–' PC Wilkins stopped. It was the most difficult case of his three years in the Mitrebury police force.

'How's your mother's arthritis, Timothy?'

'Very well.' Being a polite, well-reared young man, he added, 'Thank you for asking, doctor.'

'Why, there's the Wilkins lad,' came a loud greeting from the entrance under the blue lamp. Freddie fixed the policeman with his eye. 'What are you doing with Dr Hill?'

PC Wilkins drew himself up. 'I have reason to suspect that he has over the legal limit of alcohol in his body.'

'And *we* have reason to suspect that we have over the legal limit of alcohol in *our* bodies,' Freddie informed him genially.

'But you're not in charge of a motor vehicle,' PC Wilkins pointed out.

'We've all been to a vale ... valedic ... farewell dinner,' Roland told him. 'Do you know who was the chairman? Sledgehammer McTavish, your very own chief constable.'

PC Wilkins stopped himself from impulsively coming to attention.

'We left the stupid b arguing over the bill,' Freddie reflected. 'I hope he leaves ten p under the plate.'

Biggin yawned more deeply. 'I really must be getting along. Don't bother about the coffee, Timothy.'

'Yes, toddle off to beddy-byes, all of us,' agreed Roland.

'Good night, young fellow.' Freddie put his arm round PC Wilkins' shoulders. 'I'll give you a day's fishing some time. You're a

94

handy young scallywag with a trout fly, if I remember.'

'Dr Hill!' All three stopped at the doorway, startled by the command in the policeman's voice. He took a deep breath. 'Under the Road Traffic Act 1972, Section 5,' he recited quickly, 'I suspect you of the offence of driving or attempting to drive a motor vehicle on a road or other public place when unfit to drive, through the action of drink or drugs.'

The three stared in amazed silence.

'I must ask you to take a breathalyser test, Dr Hill,' he continued quietly, producing a square tin box from under the counter.

'Breathalyser test?' exclaimed Roland.

'If you're going to breathalyse him, you're going to breathalyse *us*,' Freddie declared doughtily. 'We're the Three Musketeers. All for one and one for all.'

'Athos!' pronounced Roland, slapping his chest.

'Porthos!' declared Freddie, grabbing a ruler from the desk and making duelling thrusts towards PC Wilkins' midriff.

'Dear me, who *was* the other one?' murmured Biggin. 'Harris? No, that's in *Three Men in a Boat*. I've got it! Aramis. Yes, I'm Aramis,' he exclaimed, looking pleased with himself.

PC Wilkins was assembling a pair of breathalyser bags. Freddie grabbed them from the counter. 'One for you and one for me,' he directed Roland. 'One, two, three, blow!'

The two doctors blew, as if squeakers at a New Year's party. PC Wilkins silently assembled a third, which he passed to Biggin. 'Doctors, I–' He gulped. 'I can arrest you for drunk and disorderly behaviour.'

Freddie and Roland exchanged glances. The evening was acquiring the unbelievable grotesqueness of a horror movie on the telly. 'Arrest us?'

'And for obstructing the police in the execution of their duty,' PC Wilkins added in one breath.

'Remember when we treated young Timothy here for chickenpox?' Freddie demanded loudly.

'A disgusting sight he was, too,' Roland agreed heartily.

'And the flits?'

'And the truancy. Remember, Timothy?' said Roland. 'We gave your mother a certificate. Said you were suffering from school phobia. You'd nothing of the kind, of course. You were bone idle. Otherwise–'

'You'd have been in trouble with the

police,' Freddie said briskly.

They were interrupted by a loud hiccup. 'Can't blow mine up at all,' Biggin complained.

'Get Dr Hill a glass of water, Timothy, there's a good lad,' Roland directed.

Timothy hesitated. But the deference which he had felt since childhood towards Mitrebury's most respected and most endearing doctors overcame his sense of constabulary duty. He disappeared to the police-station kitchen.

'I really must try and blow it up,' Biggin murmured. 'If only to please Timothy.'

'Oh, I'll do it for you,' Freddie offered generously, puffing hard into the bag. 'Why don't we make him laugh?' he suggested to Roland. 'That's the infallible cure for hiccups.'

'As a matter of fact, someone told me a jolly funny story during the dinner,' Roland agreed heartily. 'How did it go now? Ah, yes. There was this girl, you see. A debutante type.'

'They don't have debutantes any more,' Biggin objected, hiccuping loudly.

'It happened years ago,' Roland explained. 'This girl went to her doctor and said that her boy-friend was rather ... well ... you know.'

'What?' Freddie demanded.

'Slow. Off the mark.'

'Go on,' said Freddie. 'I see.'

'So the doctor said, "Give him a dozen oysters for supper".'

Biggin looked puzzled. 'Oysters is amorous,' Roland told him.

'Lobsters is lecherous,' Freddie added.

'But she came back to the doctor the next day–' Roland started giggling. 'And she said to the doctor, "Doctor"–' He slapped his thigh, laughing loudly. '"Doctor, only ten of them worked".'

The other two stared at him.

'Only ten of them worked,' Roland repeated.

'Perhaps I'd better tickle him instead,' Freddie decided.

'Here's Timothy with the water,' Biggin said. 'Don't I drink out of the wrong side of the glass, or something? Oh dear, it is rather dripping down my collar.'

'I know what he needs,' exclaimed Roland. 'A shock.'

'He's got one,' observed Freddie, as 'Sledgehammer' McTavish marched into the police station.

PC Wilkins came to attention like a Buckingham Palace sentry spotting the royal car.

'What's going on here?' asked McTavish in a Clydeside accent. He was a vast, threatening, dark, heavy-jowelled man wearing Scottish evening dress with kilt, sporran, silver-buckled shoes and skean-dhu stuck in the top of his tartan stocking. Freddie thought he looked like an advertisement for instant porridge.

'I recognized your Bentley outside, Biggin—' McTavish stopped. His eyes fell on the three breathalyser bags, all their indicators bright green.

'I see,' he said gravely. 'Well? Which of you was driving?'

'Oh, I was driving,' Biggin replied amiably. 'Sorted out the bawbees at the Bishop's Arms?'

McTavish grasped him powerfully by the shoulder. 'I'm sorry. I'm very, very sorry.'

'But I can't possibly be drunk,' Biggin objected.

'And why not?' McTavish demanded sternly.

'Because this very morning I started my retirement job, as medical officer to the Mitrebury Temperance Home of Rest.'

McTavish gave a long, sorrowing sigh. 'The law must take its course. What's your name?' he demanded of PC Wilkins, who was quivering like a sapling in a rising wind.

'Wilkins, sir,' he managed to say.

'Well, you know police routine. What do you do?'

'Er ... send for the police surgeon, sir.'

'We are the police surgeons,' Freddie informed them jovially.

PC Wilkins grabbed a clipboard from the counter. 'Not according to the roster, sir. Police surgeon on duty tonight is Dr L Drake.'

'Och aye,' McTavish recalled. 'One of our two new fellers. I don't know much about them. Their names arrived on my desk this morning, with a lot of other bumf. Well, go on, PC Wilkins,' he said shortly. 'Ring up this Drake chap, that's what he gets paid for.'

He was aware of the three doctors struggling to suppress laughter, like school-boy's in the headmaster's study. His heavy eyebrows collided. 'I pride myself on my sense of humour,' the chief constable pronounced. 'But I fail to see anything in the slightest funny in that.'

'I say–!' Biggin looked round in surprise. 'It *must* have been funny. It's cured my hiccups.'

10

Lucy and Fay had discovered they could diagnose Mr Windows' mood from his tunes on the harmonium. *Rock of Ages* indicated disgruntlement. *For Those in Peril on the Sea,* a man pushed to the limits of his temper. *All is Safely Gathered in, Ere the Winter Storms Begin* – suggesting prize marrows at the altar rails and the similar succulent decorations of Harvest Festival – signified contentment. *As Pants the Hart for Cooling Streams* meant he was waiting for the pubs to open, and *Knees up Mother Brown* that he was drunk.

That night he was playing *Soldiers of the Queen,* proclaiming enthusiasm for serving the Old Chapterhouse Surgery under new mistresses. The two doctors themselves were in the sitting-room, trying to disregard the music as lighthouse-keepers the familiar distraction of the sea.

Lucy was reading the *Lancet* on the sofa. Fay was searching through the practice library in the tall bookcase. 'Ah, the *Medical Annual,*' she exclaimed. 'Just what I need–'

She inspected it. 'For 1948,' she added in disappointment. 'Do you suppose *Pig Farming for Pleasure and Profit* would be worthwhile reading?'

'Mum Arkdale told me that Dr Fellows-Smith really wanted to be a vet, but started the wrong course by mistake. Apparently he didn't find out until he was half-way through.'

Fay flopped on the sofa, picking up the *Mitrebury Echo*, running her fingers through her long hair. 'Why does nothing ever happen to Mitrebury after six o'clock in the evenings?'

'Respectability. They're hooked on it. The Mitrebury vice. If we stay long enough, we'll turn into pillars of local society, like our three predecessors. It's as inevitable as Lot's wife into a pillar of salt.'

'What did we used to do in the evening? Discos, movies, dinner with lovely men? I'm suffering from sexual amnesia,' Fay complained. 'I'm beginning to forget what it's like.'

'Weren't you chatting up that beautiful clerical thing from St Michael and All Angels? Unmarried, too.'

'And likely to stay that way. He's as queer as a curate's egg.'

Lucy threw down the *Lancet*. 'I can't understand it – not even a postcard from dear Roddy in Los Angeles.'

'Dear Roddy! I don't know how you managed to tolerate his adolescent acne.'

'He had a bumpy skin, that's all,' Lucy objected sharply.

'It must have been like going to bed with a nutmeg grater.'

'It was not!'

'There you are, arguing again.'

'I am *not*.' Lucy stopped, staring dreamily at the stuffed pheasant. 'Do you know how I first got interested in him? It was during the path course at St Boniface's. We were assigned to the same post mortem. It was cirrhosis of the liver,' she recalled tenderly. 'He asked me out. We went to that cheap Italian restaurant, opposite Casualty. We ordered *fegato*, because it sounded yummy. It turned out Italian for liver. How we laughed!'

'By now, dear Roddy has probably married a lean, suntanned Californian girl and joined the Elks,' Fay said discouragingly.

'Why is it,' Lucy demanded, 'that the only remotely possible men we meet in Mitrebury seem frightened to death of us?'

'Always the same with women doctors.'

103

'I should have thought they'd have found us interesting.'

'Only gruesome. By the time men are confident to be our intellectual equals, they've had families for years. It's quite a problem.'

'So we're staying in this practice till we hit the menopause? Unmarried, unloved and unmolested,' Lucy despaired.

'Plenty of pairs of women doctors work together for a lifetime, perfectly happily.'

'Fay, dear – and I thought you were so sophisticated.' They were interrupted by a loud knock. Both were aware that the harmonium had ceased and the telephone had rung. 'Dr Drake,' announced Mr Windows impressively. 'You're wanted by the police. At the High Street station.'

Lucy leapt up. 'Oh, how thrilling! I've been longing to do my police surgeon's act. Do you suppose it'll be all Agatha Christie? A body with a dagger of strange, Oriental design in the back? Though of course, the butler did it.'

'Nothing so glamorous, doctor,' Mr Windows disillusioned her. 'They have some drunk person in charge of a motor-car.'

'I've absolutely no sympathy with that sort of case,' Lucy declared severely. 'Alcohol is the leading cause of death and injury on the roads. Statistics prove it.' The telephone rang again in the waiting-room. 'At least, it breaks the monotony.'

'Even a policeman with flat feet would break the monotony,' said Fay.

'Dr Liston–' Mr Windows reappeared. 'That was the police again. Apparently the drunk man is allowed under the law to have his own doctor present, when the blood is withdrawn for the alcohol test. And that is you, doctor.'

Fay looked puzzled. 'What's the patient's name?'

'They didn't say, doctor. The policeman on the telephone seemed somewhat distracted. Here are your bags. I have furnished them with syringes.'

'I suppose I'm to try and prove him sober?' Fay asked Lucy.

'And I'm to try and prove him drunk? Shall we go in my car?'

It took three minutes to the police station. 'Isn't that Dr Hill's Bentley?' Lucy said, as they hurried under the blue lamp.

'And isn't that Dr Hill?' exclaimed Fay inside. 'Quite a party,' she added, as Freddie and Roland greeted them boisterously.

'Who are you?' demanded McTavish fiercely.

'The police surgeons,' Lucy told him.

His eyebrows shot upwards like a pair of electrocuted caterpillars. 'But you're *women*.'

'And who are you?' Fay asked.

He squared his broad shoulders. 'I am the chief constable.'

'Oh, sorry. I thought you were the prisoner.'

'Police surgeons! Young flibbertigibbets.'

Lucy eyed him coolly. 'We are doctors who are perfectly entitled to practise. Or would you like to see our licence?'

'And I never even agreed with police-women,' he muttered, looking round the bleak room. 'With their little round hats and their shoulder-bags and little check ties and black tights.'

'*I'm* your patient,' said Biggin.

'But he's the soberest one in the room.' Lucy thought how tired and bemused he looked.

'I'm going home,' McTavish announced. 'Thank God I'm a bachelor. You know the routine, PC Wilkins? The blood specimen must be divided into two portions. One for the police laboratory, the other for the accused. You can have it independently analysed, if you wish,' he told Biggin, grasping him again by the shoulder. 'I'm sorry this had to happen, old man. But the law is the law. It's above either of us, isn't it?'

'I think I'm getting my hiccups again. Perhaps it was the frozen prawns?' Biggin suggested. 'I did make a bit of a beast of myself with them,' he admitted mildly. 'And they were probably Mongolian, or something. Not like the old days, when they sold them by the pint, fresh from Yarmouth, and the fishmonger wore a straw boater.'

'I'll give you two fellows a lift home.' McTavish interrupted Biggin's reminiscences. 'I had the sense to order a car, with a driver.'

'Yes, on the rates,' Freddie told him.

'Good-night ladies, Good-night ladies,' Roland sang, kissing the two young doctors heartily.

'See you in the morning, Biggin,' Freddie added. 'And we'll all have a damn good laugh about this nonsense. C'mon.'

The three doctors were left alone with PC Wilkins. 'It is a nonsense,' Biggin protested mildly. 'I had nothing more than one shandy gaff.'

'That's what they all say,' PC Wilkins murmured to himself.

Lucy unclipped her bag. 'I'm afraid you'll have to take off your jacket and roll up your left shirt-sleeve, Dr Hill.'

'But the funny thing is,' he continued, obeying her. 'All I feel is the need of a stiff drink.'

11

Freddie and Roland arrived at the Old Chapterhouse Surgery early the following morning. They needed treatment more urgently than any of the patients.

Mr Windows was waiting to give it. On the sitting room table were arranged the eggs, the tomato juice, the tabasco, the Worcester sauce, the red pepper, the tin of liver salts. His hangover cure was famous among the officers and passengers borne by Britain's Merchant Navy across the Seven Seas.

'Good morning, doctors.' Mr Windows cracked the eggs into a pair of tumblers. 'I ascertained from the lady doctors all that transpired in the police station last night.'

Roland held a hand across his eyes. 'Someone seems to have burgled my skull and tied a knot in my optic chiasma.'

Freddie gripped his abdomen. 'Must have been mad. Mixed liqueur brandy and vintage port. Ravages my gall-bladder.'

'Take your medicine, doctors.' Mr Windows presented two foaming glasses on a salver. 'The mixture as before.'

Their choking noises turned into a long sigh of relief as the therapy took effect. Freddie had for years tried to analyse the pharmacological effect of Mr Windows' potion. He decided that the furnace feeling in the stomach took the mind off the hangover. They looked up as the two young doctors came in, just finished morning surgery.

'Well! You two were flying nicely last night,' Fay greeted them pleasantly.

'The older you get.' Freddie grumbled, 'the more you develop a tolerance for people and the less for alcohol.'

'I'm suffering from total amnesia,' Roland confessed.

'All I remember,' said Freddie, 'we seemed to rub McTavish's sporran up the wrong way.'

'Then I must remind you,' Lucy said more seriously. 'Dr Hill will be in court on a drink-driving charge.'

Roland nodded, recollecting. 'Bad Luck, of course. But it's happening all the time. To politicians, actors, lawyers. Quite a club.'

'Though isn't it sad?' asked Fay, matching Lucy's mood. 'After thirty-five years as a dignified Mitrebury doctor?'

'Always kept his nose clean, old Biggin

110

Hill,' Freddie reflected. 'Even during the war, at that WAAF depot. He only committed one indiscretion, and he married her.'

'He won't only lose his licence, but his job,' Fay pointed out. 'In the Temperance Rest Home, he'll smell like grilled chops to vegetarians.'

'That job means a lot to him,' Freddie agreed. 'Otherwise, he'd have nothing to do, but stay at home and talk to his wife. I for one see his point,'

'We've got to get him out of it,' decided Roland.

'How?' asked Freddie.

'If I may make so bold,' suggested Mr Windows, 'by extracting his blood specimen from the police.'

'That would be highly unprofessional,' Lucy dismissed it brusquely.

'Come on. Be a sport,' urged Fay.

'A sport?' she asked in horror. 'May I remind you that we are police surgeons?'

'You're a prig,' said Fay. 'I am not!'

'Yes, you are. An argumentative, prissy prig.'

'Not arguing again, surely?' Liz Arkdale bustled through the door. 'Personally, I don't care if you gouge each other's eyes out, but the patients don't care to hear their doctors behaving quite as ill-manneredly as their Members of Parliament. It destroys confidence. Why not employ some catch-word inhibition to break it up? Like Pavlov's dog, you know. Let's say—'

'Pax?' said Lucy flippantly, crossing her fingers.

'Jolly hockey-sticks?' suggested Fay.

'"Hippocrates"' would sound more pro-fessional. Yes, whenever you feel a row com-ing on, say, "Hippocrates" to each other.'

'Yes, Mrs Arkdale,' said Fay meekly.

'Well. Go on.'

'Hippocrates,' said Fay to Lucy.

'Hippocrates,' said Lucy to Fay.

Both giggled. Liz Arkdale turned her attention to the older doctors, who were sitting on the sofa with their heads in their hands. 'I heard the whole story of last night while I was operating at the Infirmary. It's all round Mitrebury, of course.'

'What a place for gossip,' Freddie groaned. 'Do you remember when one of the canons desecrated the bus shelter?'

'Our argument, Mrs Arkdale,' Lucy explained stiffly, 'was because Fay actually suggested that we somehow got Dr Hill's blood specimen back from the police.'

'What a super idea,' she said.

'Mrs Arkdale! But it would be on my conscience.'

'You're just being toffee-nosed,' Fay exclaimed.

'I most certainly am not.'

'Of course you are.'

'Hippocrates,' said Mrs Arkdale.

'Hippocrates,' said Fay, after a moment.

'Hippocrates,' said Lucy.

'Supposing Mr McTavish *gave* it back?' Liz suggested. 'If it was on anybody's conscience, then it would be on his own.'

'Some chance,' Roland objected, 'with his Presbyterian sense of duty.'

'Remember when I shot that sheep by mistake?' Freddie recalled. 'He'd have hanged me, had our local magistrates given their permission.'

'It might be worth a gentle plea,' Liz decided.

'He wouldn't even see us,' Fay retorted bleakly. 'He regards women as a menace just short of smallpox. Poor Dr Hill!'

'He is such a darling,' Lucy said.

'Expelled from the Temperance Home,' added Roland gloomily.

'Branded as felon,' said Freddie.

'Perhaps I'll think of something,' suggested Liz more hopefully.

Westshire Police Headquarters was a four-storey stone building, square as a fort, off the London road on the outskirts of Mitrebury. Beyond, the modern, white drug factory, whose chairman had interrogated Lucy and Fay, sprawled across the green fields like a vast milking parlour. Beyond that, was a base which the Americans had never abandoned since their Flying Fortresses and Liberators whirred into the air to Cologne and Hanover, and from which fighter-planes now spasmodically screamed into the inoffensive sky, to the weary irritation of the Mitrebury inhabitants.

At noon that morning, a young policeman tapped on the door of the chief-constable's office. Deferentially laying a chit on the spotless blotter of the glistening desk, he announced, 'A lady to see you, sir.'

Sledgehammer McTavish scowled at the pass. 'Aye, Mrs Elizabeth Arkdale. The woman telephoned me. I suppose I had better pay for my own foolishness in agreeing to see her. Show her in.'

The only decoration of the office was a photograph of McTavish in kilt and singlet competing at the Highland Games, and a portrait in oils of a robed and wigged judge, whose expression made Judge Jeffrey's look like Dr Barnardo.

'Good morning, Mrs Arkdale,' he said with fearsome cold politeness, as the young policeman held open the door for her. 'I observe that your pass explains your business as "personal". It is not my practice to discuss personal matters in police time. *You* know that, don't you, constable?'

'Yes, sir,' he replied smartly.

'But as you're here,' McTavish conceded with an arrogant sweep of his hand, 'you'd better take a seat.'

'Thank you, chief constable.' Liz demurely took the edge of a glistening black leather armchair.

'Very well,' he commanded the policeman, 'you may go.'

The door shut. McTavish underwent a change comparable to a snowball in an atomic pile.

'Liz–' He jumped from his chair, fell on his knees, seized her hand, pressed it to his lips. 'What a wonderful surprise! My, you're looking bonny. Bonnier than ever.'

'Thank you, Sandy,' murmured Liz, offering a cheek to supplement her fingers. 'You always did know how to flatter a woman.'

He opened the door of a cupboard under

a case of legal books. 'A wee dram?' He produced bottle, glasses and a tartan-coloured tin. 'A single malt. Very old. Very special.'

'I'll just have a shortbread,' Liz informed him. 'I'm driving.' He opened the tin. 'H'm, petticoat tail,' she observed knowledgeably.

'And how's your husband?'

'Very well.'

McTavish made an emotional noise, resembling air escaping rapidly from a balloon. 'Just to think, Liz! I could have been your husband.' He stared down at his glistening toe-caps. 'But I was too shy to ask, wasn't I?'

Liz arched an eyebrow. 'I hope that wasn't the only reason?'

'No,' he admitted fairly. 'There was my mother. She had such a low opinion of Sassenachs.'

Liz nodded towards the framed photograph. 'The real answer, Sandy, was your being much more fond of tossing your caber.'

His face suffused with a look which would have startled equally the criminals and police of Mitrebury. 'It's our little secret, isn't it, Liz? It's our memory, as soft, as warm...' He searched for appropriate poetry. 'As the morning sun breaking through the fret in the glen.'

'Sandy, you're sometimes quite over-poweringly romantic,' Liz told him, adding, 'Like your Scots scenery.'

'I'll admit, there's no place in the world like it,' he exclaimed candidly. 'Well, what can I do for you?' His air suggested that law and order in Mitrebury would he suspended until he had attended her wishes.

'Dr Hill,' Liz said.

There was a pause. 'I had to do my duty, Liz.'

'Of course you did, Sandy,' she told him gently. 'If only other men had half your dedication to their work! Which includes backing up your two new police surgeons.'

'I will back them to the hilt if they deserve it. Even if they are mere girls.'

'They do deserve it. They're qualified doctors, exactly like Dr Hill and his partners. The only difference is their being several times more competent.'

'I always reserve my opinion of anyone – man or woman – until they've proved themselves.'

'Only one thing they lack, Sandy. Confidence. And you could so easily give it them.'

McTavish considered this suggestion. 'Shall I send them a box of chocolates?'

'Call on them for a chat. You did with the old doctors often enough.'

He looked uneasy. 'I wouldn't care to show favouritism.'

Liz seemed amazed. 'Favouritism? But nobody could accuse a man so strong as you of that weakness.'

He admitted frankly, 'I know my own mind. Nobody can deny it. Well, perhaps I'll pay a courtesy call. Just to please you, Liz.'

She rose. 'Good. Seven this evening? They'll have finished surgery. Not a word that I suggested it. You darling man. Now I must fly. I'm already keeping a Caesar waiting.'

She kissed him. He was left standing in the middle of the room, wearing an expression of what might have been, that would have fitted the defeated and exiled Bonnie Prince Charlie.

12

The Old Chapterhouse Surgery had the air of a village hall shortly before the ceremonial arrival of the Queen.

'But *why's* he coming?' Lucy asked Fay, as Mr Windows spiritedly performed *The Campbells are Coming* on his harmonium.

'It's obvious. He's had second thoughts about Dr Hill. He's going to tell us to forget about last night, just as completely as Drs Fellows-Smith and Carmichael seem to have done.'

'I suppose it hasn't occurred to you that he's just coming to fire us?'

'But we haven't done anything wrong,' Fay objected.

'Of course we have. Being born female.'

Mr Windows broke off opening the box marked *Resuscitation*. 'Doctors, I took the liberty of purchasing from the off-licence a bottle of Auld Killiecrankie on the practice expenses. The chief constable's favourite tipple, I am assured by the late doctors. And if I may counsel – no water. And particularly *no ice*. Mr McTavish responds to ice in his whisky more violently than to a slug in his salad.'

The doorbell clanged.

'My rabbit's foot!' Fay felt in her dress.

'You're wearing a bra,' exclaimed Lucy.

'With a man like McTavish, I feel I should be wearing a yashmak.'

The chief constable filled the doorway. Lucy wondered if she should curtsy.

'Good evening,' he said.

'Good evening,' they said.

There was a silence. He solemnly handed Mr Windows his cap and leather-bound baton.

Lucy and Fay said together, 'Perhaps you'd care to step into–' They stared foolishly at each other.

'I know how to make myself at home,' he announced, entering the sitting-room.

Lucy offered the armchair. Fay brought a stool for his feet. Lucy pressed smoked salmon sandwiches ('Tay salmon, of course'). Fay poured a large Auld Killiecrankie.

'My favourite single malt,' he exclaimed. 'Well, well. What a coincidence, your favouring it too.'

'Nothing else passes my lips,' Fay assured him.

'And I'm glad to find a woman who knows you should never drown or freeze the soul of Scots whisky,' he declared wonderingly.

The two doctors thought the evening was starting splendidly.

'Though I must admit,' he told them with a candid look, 'I do not regard police surgeon as an appropriate occupation for one of the tenderer sex. It is one liable to lead you into peril. There are some violent and nasty people in Mitrebury.'

'There were some violent and nasty people in the war,' Lucy informed him politely. 'But my father tells me that the women medical officers were magnificent.'

McTavish permitted himself to say, 'Mebbe.'

'You've come about Dr Hill, haven't you?' asked Fay, smiling.

'Such a dedicated doctor,' Lucy emphasized quickly. 'Who's done so much for Mitrebury.'

'How tragic if he lost his job,' Fay added. 'How much more if he lost his reputation.'

'What is your meaning?' McTavish's manner chilled quicker than iced whisky.

'You came to tell us that – officially – the events of last night never happened?' Fay suggested rashly.

He scowled. 'Young woman, you are becoming perilously near inviting me to pervert the course of justice.'

Lucy lost patience. 'Dr Hill was perfectly harmless. Asleep in his car at the traffic lights outside the police station.'

'Aye. Asleep with more than the permitted limit of alcohol in his blood. Dr Hill was breaking the law. Which it is my duty to administer.' In one movement, he gulped his whisky and stood up.

'Surely, you can see the difference between justice and the law?' Lucy demanded.

He glared at her. 'I canna. There is none.'

'Chief constable–' Fay drew herself up. 'The quality of mercy is not strained. Shakespeare.'

'Doctor. The best laid schemes o' mice an' *women* gang aft a-gley. Robbie Burns. Damn and blast!' he exclaimed, as a bleep came from his pocket. 'Where's the telephone?' he demanded.

He dialled, spoke briefly, scowled heavily. Fay and Lucy stared at each other, self-reproachful that they had botched the operation. He slammed back the telephone.

'Police surgeons – it is time for you to perform your duty. I'll brief you in the car.'

There was a crowd outside High Street

police station, kept away from the door by half a dozen policemen.

'Anyone left in there?' McTavish asked the nearest officer, jumping from the car followed by Fay and Lucy.

'PC Wilkins, sir.'

McTavish groaned.

'The young woman's got a shotgun?'

'That's correct, sir. She's shouting that the police are persecuting her husband.'

'What's he done?'

'Travelled on the train without a ticket.'

McTavish groaned louder.

'How'd she manage to get into a police station *with* a shotgun?' he demanded fiercely.

'In her baby's pram, sir.'

McTavish looked shocked.

'You mean, there's a wee one in there, too?'

'I'll tackle her,' said Lucy immediately. 'She's just hysterical.'

'It's no woman's work,' he told her sternly. 'I got you here to tend the wounded.'

'The coo of a dove, Mr McTavish,' Fay said emphatically, 'often works better than the bellow of a bull.'

'If she shoots herself, you'll lose your job,' he said briskly.

'If she shoots me, you'll lose yours,' Lucy returned in the same tone.

He led them up the steps. He edged open the door. Peering through the crack, Lucy saw a young woman in jeans, waving a shotgun in the direction of distraught PC Wilkins.

'Think of your mother,' he was inviting pressingly.

'I hate my mother!'

'Think of your baby,' he urged, nodding urgently towards the pram beside her.

'I haven't got one,' she said shrilly. 'That's Mrs Leary's pram. She wants it back by tomorrow morning.'

'Think of something nice.' PC Wilkins considered swiftly. 'Like the Costa Brava. Or Christmas. Or Coronation Street.'

'I want to die!' Lucy and Fay had slipped through the door. 'Who are you?' she demanded suspiciously, transferring her aim from PC Wilkins.

'We're doctors. We've come to help you,' Lucy told her gently.

'*No one* can help me.'

'Your bra strap's showing,' Fay mentioned casually.

The woman automatically looked down. PC Wilkins grabbed her. The gun clattered to the floor. McTavish sprung through the door, engulfing her and PC Wilkins in his grasp. Lucy noticed her own hands were shaking. The room was suddenly full of policemen.

Twenty minutes later, Lucy and Fay were delivered home by a police car. 'I'm still terrified,' said Lucy.

'I'm circulating undiluted adrenalin,' said Fay.

They grabbed the Auld Killiecrankie. The *Mitrebury Echo* telephoned. Mr Windows played *The Entry of the Gladiators*. The doorbell clanged. It was the chief constable.

'I shan't keep you a moment,' he declared gruffly. 'You have just performed a great service to the police, doctors.' He came into the waiting-room, saluting. 'And to humanity. At great personal risk. May I say that you are a pair of brave young women? May I say that you have proved yourselves – far more than proved yourselves – in my estimation? I am proud to have you as my police surgeons,' he told them handsomely. 'Will you please accept this as an emblem of my thanks?'

He handed Lucy a small cardboard box, saluted again and left.

'What is it?' asked Fay. 'A medal?'

'No. A bottle.'

'We shan't have much of a party on one that size.'

'We shall,' Lucy contradicted her. She held it up.

'A blood sample!'

Lucy was already on the telephone. 'Dr Hill? We've got your blood back from Mr McTavish.'

'Oh, yes,' said Biggin.

'But Dr Hill! Isn't it thrilling? Now there can't be any prosecution.'

'There couldn't be anyway,' he explained. 'I had my sample analysed urgently by my old pal Higginbotham – the biochemist at the Infirmary. No alcohol. Not a trace. Freddie blew into my bag at the police station. McTavish must have realized as much when he woke up this morning, because a shandy gaff was all I had on the bill. It was dyspepsia from the prawns. But I suppose police routine had to be followed last night, and police face saved again this morning,' he suggested knowingly. 'Old Sledgehammer's as thick as a well-boiled haggis, you know.'

'That male chauvinist double-dealing died-in-the-wool pig,' Lucy exclaimed, relaying the conversation to Fay. 'Trying hard to look human.'

Fay sighed wearily. 'Men were deceivers ever,' she quoted Shakespeare for the second time that evening.

'Mr Windows,' Lucy enquired sweetly. 'Could you play us something from the opera *Salome?*'

13

Their next row was about the new waiting-room curtains. 'But, Fay, this would be much more practical,' protested Lucy in the sitting-room before morning surgery. She waved a sample of white material, with a severe geometrical design in black.

'But, Lucy, this would be much more fun.' Fay's pattern was a jumble of reds, blues and yellows.

'Might I remind you that we're not furnishing a disco?'

'Nor an operating theatre.'

'Really, Fay! I can't see why you make a fuss about something so unrelated to medical practice as the curtains.'

'They are intimately related to medical practice. A bad doctor overlooks the psychological state of the waiting patients.'

'I am not a bad doctor. You're being insulting.'

'There you go, arguing again.'

'Hippocrates,' came from the doorway, as Liz Arkdale hurried in.

'Hippocrates,' said Lucy obediently.

'Hippocrates,' said Fay. They smiled sheepishly. It was a ridiculous invocation of their professional father.

'About time you had new curtains,' Liz told them. 'I can't remember if the old doctors had the existing ones cleaned to celebrate England winning the World Cup or the Coronation. If you're smartening up, you can do without that ducky buck on the surgery wall. And the salmon – which must have been delicious with mayonnaise, but is pushing its luck among the decorative arts. As I'm back, my first duty to Mitrebury was seeing how you're getting along.'

It was a month later, St Barnabas's Day in the middle of June. Since the night's dramatics at the police station, Liz had been on holiday at St Tropez. 'I suppose the publicity brought you a rush of patients?' she suggested.

'The publicity was somewhat diminished by the *Mitrebury Echo* discovering that the gun was unloaded, solid with rust, and had hung in the bar of the *Bishop's Arms* longer than anyone could remember,' Lucy explained.

'Ninety-four new patients have joined the practice,' Fay told Liz eagerly. 'Which more than compensates for the thirty-eight members of the Women's Institute who walked out.'

'Congratulations. All prostatic old clergymen, I suppose?'

'No, but they do seem to be suffering from the same complaint,' Lucy said.

'Oh? Is it catching?' asked Liz.

'Very.' Fay opened the door on the waiting-room, which was filling with patients.

'I see what you mean,' observed Liz. Nearly all were women, and nearly all of them in an advanced state of pregnancy. 'If you like, you can shepherd this waddling flock into my maternity unit at the Infirmary.'

'But they don't want to go into the Infirmary,' Lucy complained. 'They're set on giving birth at their own firesides.'

'Can't blame them,' agreed Liz. 'Maternity wards these days are so full of clinical machinery, they look like production lines for Hondas, not humans. Can you cope with the work?'

'We *are* two doctors doing the work of three,' Fay pointed out virtuously.

'H'm. Your predecessors were dear men, but they didn't actually give themselves hernias in the pursuit of their profession. Why not get a locum for the summer, to help you out? Then you'll be free for country rambles, or whatever you get up to.'

'But a good locum is as hard to find as a window cleaner,' said Lucy.

'I might be able to help,' Liz continued thoughtfully. 'I heard that one of my former house surgeons isn't working at the moment. Dr Janet Macgregor, she's married to an MO aboard one of those Polaris submarine things. She's the niece of Admiral Sir Hugo Hennicker-Hewson, who's got a weekend place across at Fenny Bottom. I'll give her a call in Scotland. Now I've got to turn some breech babies bottoms up. Must fly.'

'Why are you looking as dismal as a rubber duck with a puncture?' Lucy enquired of Mr Windows, as Liz roared away in her Ferrari.

'The last doctors had such a *gentlemanly* practice. And I am not a maternal man,' he apologized.

'It's an instinct you'll have to develop,' Fay told him cheerfully. 'Surely you've heard by now, there isn't a lot in that story about the gooseberry bush?'

'It ain't that easy,' he replied with a reminiscent look. 'I remember one ship's doctor we had, on a Caribbean cruise. Retired Naval surgeon, a fine man, straight as a spar. A lady was caught short between Trinidad and Barbados. She should never have gone in the ship's rumba competition, not in her condition,' he said disapprovingly.

'But the ship's doctor hadn't seen the parts actual, not since about the time of the Battle of Jutland. Not professionally, I mean. He wasn't half surprised when the baby's head came from where it did. He said afterwards, it reminded him of the time a puff-adder came up his bathroom plughole in Calcutta. Still, you had to laugh.'

'I think I'd better see my first patient, Mr Windows,' said Lucy firmly.

She was followed into her consulting room by a small, wispy, balding, ragged-moustached man in a neat blue suit, carrying a large old leather suitcase. Behind was a plump, scarlet-cheeked, blonde, pregnant woman.

'Your first baby, Mrs Elvis?' asked Lucy, opening the folder of notes on her desk and indicating the pair of patients' chairs.

'Yes, this is our very first,' Mr Elvis answered proudly.

'And everything is going well, Mrs Elvis?'

'Very well indeed, doctor,' replied Mr Elvis.

Lucy glared at him. 'How are you feeling in yourself?' she enquired of the wife.

'Fine,' said Mr Elvis.

'I'd better take the patient's blood pressure.' Lucy reached for the sphygmomanometer.

'One hundred and thirty over eighty-five, doctor, quite normal,' Mr Elvis' prim voice informed her. 'We have bought a machine. Japanese.'

'Which one of you is actually having the baby?' asked Lucy with curiosity.

'I am very interested in modern medicine and its miracles,' he told her solemnly. 'It is my belief that you doctors do wonderful work.'

'Thank you.'

'I too am connected with the healing profession – I am an employee of the Mitrebury sanitation department – and assure you that everything has been done to expedite the wife's delivery. I had a lucky little flutter with the Premium Bonds, which allowed me to indulge somewhat lavishly in the baby care shop in the High Street. Furthermore–' He snapped open the suitcase. 'I have this afternoon furnished myself with the literature on our condition from the public library. Happy Birthdays.' He held up a worn book. *What To Do Till the Midwife Comes. Bitches in Whelp* – oh dear, that must be from the veterinary section.'

'When are you due, Mrs Elvis?'

'On Sunday week, doctor,' Mr Elvis replied. 'Just after the late news. The nine months are then up. Precisely.'

'It's a wonder you've got time to watch television,' Lucy murmured to him. 'Or even to inspect your drains.'

'We're performing our exercises, night and morning,' Mr Elvis assured her, demonstrating.

'I hope they're doing you good?'

'Naturally, I intend to witness the actual miracle of birth,' he continued gravely. 'I believe it to be one of the most uplifting and inspiring experiences in a man's life.'

'The mother gets something out of it, too, you know. I shall want a specimen–'

Mr Elvis produced from his suitcase a quart cider bottle, filled to the stopper.

'Generous, if not elegant.' Lucy took it, asking him, 'Yours, I suppose?'

Mrs Elvis started to giggle. 'It's all mine,' she corrected her medical attendant. 'Down to the last drop.'

It was during surgery a week later that Lucy noticed a gingery woman in an expensive maternity outfit of tweed, who was saying to Mr Windows,

'I have an appointment with Dr Drake.'

'Yes, madam,' he responded warily. 'If you'll both step this way.'

'Ah–!' The stranger's face brightened. 'You must be Dr Drake? I've a little confession to make.'

'Somewhat unnecessary, isn't it?' remarked Lucy, inspecting her.

'Hubby's boat was held up by some terribly top secret mechanical fault, and didn't put to sea till yesterday. I'm sure you'll understand how we wanted to spend as long together in Scotland as possible, before he disappears under the North Pole.'

'You're Dr Macgregor?' exclaimed Lucy in horror.

'And I can't tell you how I'm looking forward to a spell of work. I'm so glad Liz Arkdale summoned me. You get so utterly bored, with nothing to look at but the hills.' She glanced round the crowded surgery. 'And you must be Dr Liston?' she smiled, as Fay stalked across. 'I came round as soon as I'd dropped my kit in the Bishop's Arms. I'll take my watch for emergency calls, of course. I've already had a word with the night porter, though he is rather arthritic and deaf.'

'But aren't you a little...' began Fay

crossly. 'I mean ... damn it, you look as though you're going to drop it any moment.'

'Oh, *this?*' Dr Janet Macgregor's attention seemed drawn to her bulge for the first time. 'Don't worry, I'm not due till a month on Sunday. I can work it out exactly, you see, from the time my husband's submarine was in port. I'm an enthusiast for the modern doctrine of working and moving about till the last moment. And when are you due?' she asked kindly of an expectant mother with a toddler pulling her skirt.

'Next Sunday, doctor.'

'That's Mrs Burgess,' Lucy added.

'No, doctor, I'm Mrs Palmer.'

'I'm Mrs Burgess, and I'm due on Sunday,' said the one beside her.

'It seems Mothering Sunday's coming up,' murmured Fay.

'Why can't I go into action?' Janet beamed round, rubbing her hands. 'Who's next?'

'From experience, doctor,' gently replied another pregnant patient, rocking a pram with twins. 'I think it might be you.'

Lucy drew Fay aside. 'I suppose Dr Macgregor knows what she's about? She's an intelligent patient.'

'Rule one in obstetrics,' Fay replied. 'There is no such thing as an intelligent patient.'

14

'You've got work to do,' Lucy told Fay. It was the following Sunday afternoon.

'I haven't had any lunch.' Fay came into the surgery from seeing a prebendary's pneumonia.

'Neither have I. Instead, I was delivering Mrs Ramachandran – the one who always did that lovely little namasta when she came for her ante-natal. Now Mrs Burgess is on the boil. So is Mrs Palmer, if not boiling over.'

'Well? What about the midwives?'

'One's got a virus and the other's in Greece.'

The telephone rang.

'Dr Drake?' It was Mr Elvis, excited. 'We're having it. Exactly as I said. If a shade early. But I don't suppose that'll bother you?'

'Are you sure?' Lucy asked curtly.

He sounded offended. 'Of course I'm sure. I know the symptoms as well as I know the town drains. We are suffering severe backache and experiencing regular contractions. Just as described in *Having a Baby is Fun*.'

'I'll be round as soon as possible. Keep calm.'

'I am as calm as the boy upon the burning deck, doctor. I think my loved one calls. Ta Ta.'

'What the hell are we going to do?' Lucy put down the telephone, looking frantic. 'The two of us can't cope. Even if we'd as many arms as the peculiar statues round Mrs Ramachandran's bed.'

Fay snapped her fingers. 'Mum Arkdale!'

'She's been with the Duchess at Westshire Court all day, and is expecting to stay there all night. That family are stately breeders.'

'We've completely forgotten our eager helpmeet, Janet,' Fay exclaimed.

'Of course! She hasn't examined the cases, but women give birth on the bus when they haven't been previously examined by the conductor. We'll tell her it's all hands to the pumps,' Lucy said cheerfully.

'Ring the ducal delivery-room anyway,' Fay advised. 'We may still need Mum Arkdale to throw us an obstetrical lifebelt.'

Janet Macgregor was sitting amid the brassware and sporting prints of the lounge at the Bishop's Arms, feet comfortably on a pouffe, sipping her after-lunch coffee and watching racing on the television.

'Work? Splendid!' She rose from her armchair. 'I was bracing myself for a terribly dull weekend–'

She stopped, gasped and held her back.

'All right?' asked Lucy alarmed.

'Not backache?' asked Fay, more so.

'Just a twinge.' Janet smiled. 'I pulled something, shifting my window this morning. I don't think it's been opened since the days of Dick Turpin.' Noticing the expressions of her companions, she exclaimed, 'Oh, *backache!* Don't worry about *that*. I'm not due for a whole month yet. Where do you want me to perform?'

'A Mrs Elvis, in the housing estate off the London road,' Lucy informed her, 'Should be perfectly straightforward.'

'The husband might be difficult,' Fay warned.

'Yes,' agreed Lucy. 'If God hadn't done that stuff with Adam's rib, Mr Elvis could have populated the world all by himself.'

Mr and Mrs Elvis had a white-walled, red-roofed semi-detached house with a neat front garden. Twenty minutes later, Janet Macgregor with her bag of instruments pushed open its pink gate painted 'Kumincyde.' Mr

Elvis threw wide the front door, He wore a green surgical gown and cap, a surgical mask dangling below his chin, his hands in rubber gloves.

'You're the doctor?' Janet asked at once.

'Oh, no, doctor. You're the doctor,' Mr Elvis corrected her.

'Do you always wear that sort of thing about the house?'

Mr Elvis laughed. 'Got to be dressed right for my great moment, haven't I?'

'I'm Dr Macgregor. I'm standing in for Dr Drake. She's already on a case.'

Janet entered the narrow hall, which contained a set of model trains, a toy tractor, a striped beach-ball and a shiny pram with a canopy. She frowned. 'How many have you already?'

'This is our very first,' he explained proudly. 'I have everything prepared, down to the last nappy-pin. I defy anything to go wrong.' Janet winced and held her back. 'You all right, doctor?' he asked with concern.

'Just a twinge.' She smiled reassuringly. 'I ricked myself.'

'Why, doctor! You've been taking the same medicine as the wife.'

'But I'm not having mine for another four weeks. Let's see the patient.'

Mr Elvis led her upstairs with the air of Rembrandt conducting an important visitor to his studio.

The bedroom was small, the bed large, with a pink muslin drape at the head. The room was crammed with cheerfully-painted products of the maternity stores in Mitrebury High Street. Mrs Elvis' bright pink face lay on a pink pillow, her blonde hair in two substantial plaits.

'Sorry Dr Drake couldn't come herself,' Janet apologized. 'But you're not the only pregnant lady in Mitrebury.'

'So I see, doctor,' agreed Mrs Elvis.

'I have the complete baby's bottle sterilizing set.' Mr Elvis proudly indicated the glassware on the white painted dressing-table. 'Food blender,' he pointed out, taking no notice of his wife. 'Baby's bath. Baby's cot. Baby's potty. It is husbandly duty, doctor, to provide all that she may require for the great moment.'

'I couldn't half do with a cup of tea,' came from the bed.

'Tea, my love? Oh, no, my love. Nothing by mouth. That's right, isn't it, doctor?'

'I'm sure everything will go like an express train through a tunnel.' Janet opened her case on the pink plastic baby's bath.

'I've got pains, doctor.'

'Pains, my love? Quite normal. Soon now we shall he witnessing the wonderful miracle of birth.'

'I don't know which of us is going to enjoy it the most,' Mrs Elvis told him doubtfully.

'Just relax, my love. Take deep breaths. You're in the very best of hands. Talcum powder, doctor? If you need any, I got six dozen wholesale.' He upended a tin, producing a choking white cloud.

'Let's listen to the baby's heart,' Janet said patiently. She pulled back the bedclothes, raised Mrs Elvis' pink transparent nightie and applied her ear to a foetal stethoscope like an upturned flower-vase.

'Testing, testing, one, two, three, four, over to you, Roger and out,' chanted Mr Elvis. He held up a plastic microphone. 'Trying the new baby alarm.'

'Mr Elvis, would you please go to the kitchen and fetch me some boiling water?'

'I've thought of that! It's on the gas.' He became entangled with a quacking duck on wheels.

'I don't really need any hot water,' Janet told her patient as he left, 'but it seemed the only way we could have a chat in peace.'

'I don't know what Edgar's going to do

after this baby comes, honest I don't,' Mrs Elvis confessed. 'It'll be such an anti-climax. He always was such a one for gadgets. He almost knocked the house down last year with his electric drills.'

'Ouch,' said Janet.

'Doctor–!' Mrs Elvis propped on her elbow.

'It's nothing. Nothing. A slight strain. My window stuck.'

The patient's eyes narrowed. 'You're not going to beat me to it, are you, doctor?'

'Of course I'm not,' Janet said sharply. 'Absolutely out of the question. I've another whole month to run yet. Er ... did I notice a telephone in your hall?'

15

Steam came in clouds from the kitchen. Mr Elvis was inside, singing loudly *Yes Sir, That's My Baby*. Janet gripped the banisters at the foot of the stairs. She bit her lip. She held her back. She reached for the telephone and dialled.

Admiral Sir Hugo Hennicker-Hewson was enjoying a lazy Sunday at his house in Fenny Bottom.

'There's an urgent phone call, dear,' his wife shouted into the garden.

'Really?' he asked genially. 'I wasn't expecting any news likely to disturb a game of bowls on Plymouth Hoe.'

'It's Janet.'

'Probably cadging some outrageous favour.' He took the telephone. 'Hello, me love. Keeping an even keel?'

'Uncle–' came a strained voice. 'Are you commanding the fleet?'

'No, I'm putting in my onions.'

'Was HMS *Broadside* – you know, our submarine – in harbour during October last, or

144

September last?'

'September. Why?'

'Are you sure?'

'Of course I'm sure. I'm paid to remember.'

'Oh, my God.'

The telephone went dead. 'Odd,' said the admiral. 'What is it to Janet, when the fleet puts to sea?'

At 'Kumincyde', Janet leant against the wall as Mr Elvis appeared with a stewpan of steaming water, using a nursing bra as a jolly molly.

'Anything wrong, doctor?'

'I would seem to have made a slight error in navigation.'

He looked confused. 'What shall I do with the water?'

'Oh, that's not nearly enough. I must have unlimited water. Lots and lots of water. Stay in the kitchen until you've filled every receptacle in the house.'

Janet tightened her lips, and dialled the surgery. Mr Windows answered.

'Dr Macgregor here. Where are the doctors?'

'Dr Drake's at Mrs Burgess, Dr Liston's at Mrs Palmer. It's maternity fireworks day, everything going off at once.'

'Tell one doctor she's needed at Mr Elvis'. Any one. At once.'

'Complications, doctor?'

'Yes. Unknown in the history of obstetrics. 'Don't *sing*,' she complained, slamming down the telephone, as *Abide With Me* came over the line.

Janet fingered the Royal Navy brooch on the lapel of her tweed maternity suit. 'A doctor *never* lets a patient down.' She drew herself upwards by the handrail. 'Action stations,' she said resolutely. 'Even if holed below the waterline.'

'Quick!' screamed Mrs Elvis from the bed. 'I think it's coming.'

Janet leant against the doorpost. 'So do I.'

'What? You're as far gone as I am?'

'Well, we're all ready for the miracle,' said Mr Elvis brightly, coming into the bedroom with a pair of steaming plastic buckets.

'Mr Elvis – you know a lot about delivering babies, don't you?'

'I think I might say, doctor, that I have grasped the rudiments.'

'Well, you're shortly going to grasp a lot more.'

'Oh, my Gawd.' He tripped over the duck, making it quack. 'You mean, you–? Oh, my Gawd!'

146

He started feverishly turning pages of *The Joy of Childbirth*.

'Why not come and lie down, doctor?' Mrs Elvis patted the bed beside her.

'I think I will. Thank you, Mrs Elvis.'

'Call me Elsie.'

'Do you expect it'll be one at a time, or both together?' asked Mr Elvis desperately.

'Mine's eased a bit, doctor.'

'Please call me Janet, Elsie. Yes, so's mine.'

'I've had enough advice from Edgar these last nine months, I could give birth to a baby elephant.'

'I suppose it is a simple, natural process,' Janet said hopefully.

'I saw on the telly, how in China the women just go into the fields and have them. Then they go straight hack to picking the rice. *They* don't need all this maternity junk,' Mrs Elvis said scornfully.

'I don't half feel queer,' announced Mr Elvis. He slowly collapsed, with his head in the pink plastic pot.

'There you go again!' his wife exclaimed angrily. 'Letting me down in a crisis. It was just the same last summer, when our rowing boat sprang a leak at Eastbourne. We'd have been drowned and washed up on the shingle, if I hadn't taken off my tights and stuffed them in the hole.'

'Now there's three patients in the room,' Janet complained. 'It really is bloody inconvenient.'

'Oh, don't bother yourself. He often has these turns when he's overexcited.'

'And any minute there's going to be five patients– Listen!'

It was a sound familiar to Janet, from her spell as house surgeon at the Mitrebury Infirmary. The approach of a powerful car, the screech of tyres, the slam of a door. The doorbell chimed. Mrs Elvis reached for a large jug of orange juice at her bedside, and threw it over Mr Elvis.

'Wake up, you lazy sod,' she said.

'Where am I?' Mr Elvis held his head. 'You're both still here? I thought it was some terrible dream. I wish I'd never started all this in the first place.' The bell chimed again. He struggled to his feet. 'Who do you suppose it is?' he asked bemusedly. 'The man for the rent?'

'Any pair of hands would be welcome,' gasped Janet, holding her sides.

Twenty seconds later, Liz Arkdale hurried into the room, bag in hand. The doorbell chimed again.

'All right, coming!' Mr Elvis started downstairs. 'I was getting lonely.'

Another twenty seconds, and Lucy hurried into the bedroom with her bag. The doorbell chimed.

'Oh, my Gawd,' grumbled Mr Elvis, going downstairs again. 'I wonder if it's always like this?'

Twenty seconds later, Fay burst into the bedroom, bag in hand. Liz Arkdale looked round. 'At least,' she observed, 'we've got them outnumbered.'

Two hours passed. They were all drinking tea.

'Well, you've a lovely little boy, Janet,' Liz complimented one mother sitting up in bed. 'And so have you, Elsie,' she complimented the other, sitting alongside.

'I must send a signal to hubby in the Arctic Ocean,' said Janet delightedly.

'Now I'm going to drive you and young Hamish to my ward at the Infirmary.' Liz turned to Mr Elvis. 'Unless, of course, you are actually opening a maternity home?'

Mr Elvis beamed. 'The lady wife and self are very thankful for the devotion of the doctors, and I am sure that I speak for young Godric. I'm sorry I passed out at the actual miraculous moment. I am well known to be of a highly strung disposition. But all's well that ends well, eh?' He had recovered his normal optimism. 'Or as we say in the sanitation department, it doesn't matter how the sewage stinks, so long as you can drink the water.'

Lucy and Fay gave Janet a fireman's lift downstairs, Liz following with the baby.

'See you at the christening,' Mr Elvis invited at the front door. 'Thank Gawd nothing else can go wrong.'

'Edgar!' came a scream from the bedroom.

He rushed upstairs. He rushed down again with a baby. He grabbed the one from Liz in exchange.

'I think,' observed Liz, 'I shall switch into geriatrics.'

16

The bishop glanced up from his desk. 'Good morning, Arthur.'

'Good morning, my – Peter,' said his chaplain.

It was St James's Day, a Wednesday at the end of July. The Revd Arthur Dawney placed the morning post on the bishop's desk with a deep yawn.

'I hope I'm not keeping you up?' the bishop said humorously.

The chaplain took a saintly look. 'Your rebuke is well deserved.'

'It wasn't a rebuke. It was a joke.'

'Ah, I see. Another of your jokes. I did not sleep a wink last night.'

The bishop considered some remark about a clear conscience, but stifled it. 'Insomnia? Thank heavens that is unknown to me. I put my head on the pillow and there it stays for eight hours.'

'I am a martyr to sleeplessness. Dr Fellows-Smith advised me to drink a tumbler of brandy before retiring. I felt that was hardly appropriate – and the brandy, it appeared, could not be prescribed on the National Health Service. He gave me some capsules, which my wife objected made me snore all night long. However, one must tolerate certain inconveniences for the welfare of one's spouse.'

'Aren't you still taking them?' the bishop asked.

'I have run out. And I feel disinclined to consult his flighty successors.'

'Oh, come, Arthur,' the bishop protested. 'You're as bad as the chief constable. Do you realize that the next generation in Britain will find half its doctors women? In Russia it is a predominantly female profession already. Surely you must admire Mrs Arkdale, both as a gynaecological surgeon and an energetic citizen of Mitrebury? Mr Bellwether has certainly fallen quite flat under the new doctors' charm.'

'I do not believe them to be perfectly respectable.'

'That is a serious allegation.' The bishop looked stern. 'Why?'

'One of them does not wear a complete set of under clothing.'

The bishop could not help asking, 'How do you know?'

'It is a well known fact in the Theological College.' He yawned again.

'Well, you'd better find another doctor. You're making me feel quite sleepy, Arthur. I say–!' He was reading the top letter. 'I've done it! I'm going to have my own chat show. What a super way of propagating the gospel. Though a pretty miserable off-peak time-slot they've given me,' he added discontentedly.

Shortly after midday, the chaplain put on his dark trilby and left the palace. He strolled in the bright sunshine across the close towards the Old Chapterhouse Surgery. A man of his importance in Mitrebury never queued among its ordinary citizens, whether to see the doctor or to see the Australians versus Westshire. At the cricket ground he had the Lord Mayor's marquee, at the surgery an arrangement with Dr Fellows-Smith which usually carried the bonus of a lunchtime pink gin.

'I am sure the lady doctors will bestow a special consultation,' Mr Windows told him in the empty waiting-room. 'Though both are in learned discussion at the moment with a representative of a pharmaceutical company.'

The chaplain waited on a pew, hat on

knee, reading the Christmas number of *The Field* for 1976. Fay was meanwhile perched with Lucy on the desk of her consulting room, talking to a handsome man their own age. He wore a smart suit with an expensive tie, and sat relaxed in the doctor's chair, a leather case at his feet.

'But, Adam, it's so super you just turning up like this,' Lucy was saying warmly. 'After all those wonderful times all three of us had at St Boniface's.'

'And now I'm an unfrocked medical student.' He grinned. 'I don't regret in the least failing my finals and being thrown out. You can still serve humanity, you know, on a commission basis. I may only be a travelling salesman for a drug firm, but next year I'll be area manager, in five I could be running the whole country. After that Zurich, New York, Tokyo ... the sky's the limit. Top executives are expected to travel a lot, using the most luxurious hotels and entertaining lavishly at the most expensive restaurants,' he ended, looking pleased with himself

'Everyone at St Boniface's knew you'd be a success,' Fay told him admiringly. 'You were always so efficient organizing the rag week.'

Mr Windows knocked.

154

'Dr Drake, the reverend the bishop's chaplain wonders if you could fit him in a consultation special. Always scrounging favours, the clerical gents,' he mentioned to the visitor. 'You'd think they was going about with their halos and harps already.'

'I'd better see him, I suppose,' Lucy agreed unwillingly. 'I hear he can make himself a dreadful nuisance.'

As she left, Fay looked at Adam. Adam looked at Fay. They were tight in each other's arms.

'Adam, *darling*,' she gasped. 'What absolute heaven, seeing you again.'

'Fay, my sweetie,' he murmured, kissing her fiercely.

'You haven't changed.'

'And you still don't wear a bra.'

'That wonderful fortnight we had in Torremolinos.'

'Pretty torrid,' he agreed, gently biting her neck.

'Oh, Adam...' She drew herself back. 'I'm sure to see you again ... oh, I hope I'll be seeing you here lots and lots ... but not a word about Torremolinos ... or about anything else ... to Lucy.'

'I'm the soul of discretion,' he assured her, nibbling the lobe of her ear.

'I mean, it might disturb the harmony. You've simply got to get on with your partner in a medical practice, and we *do* have rows about so many stupid things.'

'Why should I share the fondest memories of my life with Lucy?' he asked, licking her eyelids.

'Lucy's absolutely sweet of course, a super girl in all respects and a first-rate doctor, but she is inclined to be bloody bitchy when she's jealous. And she's jealous of me over so many things. I can't help it if I'm cleverer than her, can I? And much better with the patients.'

He squashed her mouth against his like a schoolboy sucking an orange. They sprang apart. The door opened.

'Fay, the chaplain's your patient, as you took all Dr Fellows-Smith's list. For some reason he's shy about consulting you, but I insisted as a matter of principle.'

'You're always so correct ethically, Lucy,' Fay complimented her. 'Of course I'll see him. I should feel most upset were you doing my work for me.'

The door shut behind her. Lucy looked at Adam. Adam looked at Lucy. They were tight in each other's arms.

'Adam, my love! I'm over the moon, just

seeing you again.'

'Lucy, my angel,' he murmured, kissing her with unsapped vigour.

'You're just the same, Adam darling.'

'Your tits still turn me on like laser beams.'

'I'll never forget our week in Sorrento.'

'Sensational.'

'Oh, Adam...' She stared in alarm. 'Please, not a hint about Sorrento to Fay. She's tremendously jealous of me, you know.'

'With reason,' he murmured, massaging her thorax.

'Of course, she's a lovely girl, but utterly feckless and inclined to wicked remarks if she can find a chink in my character to slip them through.'

He pressed her mouth against his like a bandsman playing *William Tell* on the tuba. They sprang apart. The door opened.

'He only wanted a prescription for insomnia,' Fay announced. 'I gave him something with a long name but as mild as a glass of milk. I find it works by suggestion, just as well.'

Adam Vane unclipped his bag. 'I could have given you the latest thing – Superziz, we're running a million-pound marketing campaign. I'm in charge of the operation for the west of England,' he said proudly. 'Here's a supply – try it on your patients, make them instant owls. Now I'd better escape... I mean, I've got another twenty doctors to see before going back to the office.'

'Bye, Adam,' said Lucy.

'Bye, Adam,' said Fay.

'May I?' he asked respectfully.

As both young doctors demurely offered him a cheek, he chastely kissed them.

17

'Murderer,' said Lucy.

It was the next morning, and she had just come downstairs.

'What are you doing with Pasteur?' asked Fay sharply from the landing.

'Stopping it enjoying a fish breakfast.' She held at arm's length a large tabby tomcat with scarred fur and torn ears. It had strayed into the surgery, found it warm, comfortable, and providing an adequate diet, and stayed. 'Don't you give it enough of that disgusting cat food?'

'Come to mum-mums.' Fay folded it tenderly in her arms.

Lucy eyed her coldly. 'Fay, I have over the years observed you from close quarters falling in love with varied males, but your passion for that ill-tempered, noisy, smelly, intrusive feline ragbag totally baffles me.'

'And it baffled me why you spent a hundred-odd quid of the practice money on *that*.'

Beside the telephone on Mr Window's

antique desk stood an open, illuminated tank, darting with tropical fish.

'It relaxes the patients,' Lucy told her stoutly.

'Nonsense. It's just wallpaper with scales.'

'Luckily, I stopped that four-legged thug from pawing up a valuable Malayan tiger barb.'

'Pasteur has got his instincts.'

'And Pasteur has got fleas.' Lucy brushed the sleeve of her blouse.

'They're perfectly normal in active cats.' Fay kissed its head. 'I'll spray him with dichlorvos fenitrothion, if you like. But I must say, you're pathetically squeamish.'

'I care to observe elementary rules of hygiene.'

'Perhaps you should live in a sterile tent, like a heart transplant?'

'Good morning, doctors.' Mr Windows appeared from laying their breakfast in the sitting-room. 'We have two private patients at the end of surgery.'

'I should have had my hair done,' Lucy said flippantly.

'The Fanshawes. With an 'e'. A very well known Mitrebury couple. Mrs Fanshawe wishes to see the doctor at 9.45 and Mr Fanshawe at ten.'

'Aren't they coming together?' Fay asked in surprise.

'They are also a very independent couple.' Mr Windows gave a deep look. 'Your morning post, doctor. And yours.'

Lucy took the usual pile of giveaway medical journals and advertisements from drug companies. She recognized the handwriting on an envelope. 'I'll dump this rubbish in my consulting room,' she announced.

Alone, she tore open Adam Vane's letter.

Darling One,

A discreet little note to suggest a discreet little dinner. I'm back in Mitrebury this Friday. The Cordon Bleu room of the Bishop's Arms. Eight o'clock. I'll expect you. Lots of luscious love,
Adam.

Lucy's smile as she folded the note and tucked it into her bra would have fitted the face of Pasteur after consuming a tankful of fish.

Mrs Greta Fanshawe appeared promptly. She was a short, smart, pretty blonde with blue eyes and a personality which Fay thought as glitteringly determined as a gold-plated bulldozer. She was thirty-three.

'I expect you know, doctor, I'm a career

161

woman like yourself,' she began pleasantly. 'I'm managing director of Perkins Travel – you can see our new office block at Bishop's Bridge from your window. It was started by my father, Harry Perkins – people still talk about him, he was a dear friend of the old bishop, and I honestly believe worked as hard for charities as for the business. Perhaps that's why I've had to build it up with my own efforts. He died when I was twenty-one. Have you had your holiday yet, doctor?' Fay shook her head. 'I'll send you our brochure,' Greta told her promptly. 'Marakech is very popular this year, and you'll find our prices highly competitive.'

'Well, Mrs Fanshawe, what's the–' Fay broke off. 'How odd. I've lost my stethoscope, of all things.' She rummaged through the papers on her desk.

'I don't think you'll be requiring it for my case. Dr Carmichael said that my trouble is frankly psychological. I get terribly depressed and restless. I have absolutely no appetite, and headaches going on for weeks on end.'

'What did Dr Carmichael suggest?'

'That I took a holiday.'

'I suppose that is rather like telling a harassed barman to take a stiff drink. How long have you had these symptoms?'

'Six years. Since I got married.'

'Any sexual problems?' Fay asked automatically.

'Only one. My husband.'

'Oh,' said Fay.

For an instant, Greta looked uncertain of herself. 'He doesn't know I'm consulting you. He would interpret it as weakness of character. I came because I hoped a woman doctor would understand my problems better than Dr Carmichael, however charming he was.'

'I'd better examine you fully, Mrs Fanshawe.' Fay rose, indicating the couch. 'There may be a physical cause of your troubles, which we can cure. I'll have to use Dr Fellows-Smith's reserve stethoscope, which had a gallant career in World War Two, I understand.'

Lucy was saying in the next-door consulting room, 'Please sit down, Mr Fanshawe.'

'I didn't expect a lady doctor. When Mr Windows told me, I braced myself for something like the weightlifting champion of all Russia.'

'I think we have rather outgrown the butch image,' Lucy said primly.

He was slim, handsome, with chestnut hair and brown eyes. He wore sneakers, jeans and a T-shirt printed MITREBURY ART COLLEGE. He was twenty-nine, and she thought he looked like an overgrown adolescent.

'What's your name? I like informal relations with the doctor. Mine's Terry.'

'I prefer completely formal ones with the patients. Mine's Dr Drake.'

They exchanged smiles. 'Very well, Dr Drake. Not a word to my wife that I'm consulting you, I implore. You see, she dismissed me as a hypochondriac. Typical!' he exclaimed sourly. 'You must have heard of Greta in Mitrebury? She sells airline tickets to romantic places.' Lucy nodded. *'I teach at the art school, which hardly puts my income in the Picasso class. But who pays the piper – not to mention the butcher, the baker and the income-tax taker – calls the marriage dance,'* he ended resignedly.

Lucy asked his symptoms. 'Stomach pains. Generally at night.'

'What did Dr Hill advise?'

'Sleeping with the windows open. But my wife had installed terribly expensive double glazing in our cottage, so that wasn't on.'

'Will you lie on the couch, and take your shirt and trousers off?'

'In a flash,' Terry told her eagerly. 'And I

didn't mean the *double entendre,* doctor.'

Fay next door found Greta as healthy physically as a cross-Channel swimmer. She prescribed tranquillizers.

'I'll get the tablets before flying to Paris tomorrow night,' the patient said gratefully at the consulting-room door. She looked startled as Mr Windows descended on her eagerly, grabbing her briefcase and escorting her briskly towards the front entrance.

'May I carry madam's case to her car?'

'I walked, Windows. My office is hardly any distance.' It was half a mile, but she preferred not leaving her car by the surgery. Terry often ambled round Mitrebury during breaks in his classes.

Five minutes later, he appeared from Lucy's room.

'Thank you, doctor, I'm reassured I won't die in writhing agony any minute. I'll cut out the bacon and chips.' He paused, seeing Fay, who was energetically searching the drawers of Mr Windows' desk.

'My partner, Dr Liston,' said Lucy.

'Well!' Terry smiled broadly. 'The other Mitrebury doctors will soon be out of business, won't they?'

'Come back to see me if you've more pain,' Lucy instructed him.

'At the slightest twinge,' he assured her cheerfully.

'Lucy, have you got my new Japanese stethoscope?' asked Fay, as the front door closed. Lucy shook her head. 'Have *you*, Mr Windows? It was terribly expensive and fully transistorized.'

'I would not presume to use a stethoscope, doctor,' Mr Windows told her with dignity. 'I content myself with a searching glance.'

'What did you make of yours?' Fay gathered Pasteur in her arms.

'Hypochondria.' Lucy poured ants' eggs into her fish. 'Yours?'

'Neurotic. She fantasizes that her husband teaches the young ladies of Mitrebury something more exciting than drawing bowls of fruit.'

'He strikes me as pretty sexy,' Lucy said thoughtfully. 'I could hardly stop him ripping off everything, including his socks.'

'After the time we've been in Mitrebury the Hunchback of Notre Dame would strike me as pretty sexy.'

'Oh, it's so sad,' Lucy complained. 'We're so young. So desirable. So unmarried. What do we go to bed with? Hot water bottles and hot cocoa.'

'We're developing into a pair of old maids.'

166

Lucy shrugged her shoulders. 'What can we do about it?'

'Advertise for a male assistant.'

'At least, he wouldn't arrive pregnant.' She noticed the time. 'God, I'm dreadfully late to see the dean, who's immobilized with lumbago, which he puts down to draughty pulpits.'

She grabbed her medical bag from the desk and hurried out. The telephone rang as Fay was about to follow. Mr Windows stopped her.

'I have Mr Vane's secretary on the line.' He covered the mouthpiece. 'The commercial gentleman who left the new sleeping tablets in your consulting room–'

'I know, I know,' Fay told him impatiently.

'The secretary is enquiring whether the doctor will be accepting Mr Vane's invitation to dinner tomorrow night.'

'She most certainly will,' Fay said delightedly.

'It is apparently at eight o'clock. The Bishop's Arms. The Cordon Bleu room.' He added into the telephone, 'The doctor is pleased to accept.'

It was Fay's morning for the Teenage Mothers' Clinic at the bishop's palace. When she drove back for lunch, the Ferrari stood outside the surgery. Liz was in the waiting-room, listening with the interest she bestowed upon everything, to Lucy proudly displaying her angel fish, her thick-lipped gourami, bloodfins, white cloud mountain minnows and great crested newt.

'I didn't call for a piscatorial lecture,' Liz greeted Fay. 'I'm standing treat for your three predecessors tomorrow night – long overdue, they were so sweet to me all my professional life in Mitrebury. A little dinner, which I hope won't get them into such trouble as the chief constable's one. I'd love you both to join us.'

'Mrs Arkdale, how wonderful–' Lucy stopped. 'Oh! Not tomorrow night, I'm afraid.'

'Of course you can,' Fay told her.

'I'm on duty,' Lucy said quickly.

Fay looked puzzled. 'You can get your calls put through.'

'I was doing that anyway,' Lucy continued hastily. 'To the blood transfusion unit. In the Community Health Centre. I'm helping out the doctor there. I promised.'

'Oh, what a bore it's your night to play Dracula,' Liz sympathized. 'You'll come, Fay?'

'Afraid not, Mrs Arkdale.'

'Of course you can,' said Lucy forcefully. 'Only this morning you were griping that nobody asked you out anywhere, even to keep-fit classes.'

'I'm going to a lecture. At the Infirmary,' Fay asserted. 'It's advertised by the BMA. On the metabolism of heavy metals.'

'I didn't think you were interested in that,' exclaimed Lucy.

'Oh, yes. Ever since I was a student. Heavy metals are fascinating. Particularly their metabolism.'

'You're in for a cosy evening,' Liz told her. 'Just you and the lecturer. But I'm pleased that you put professional enlightenment before guzzling. Sorry I can't change the date – it's my only evening for months free of patients or committees, and my husband's being a Buffalo. Perhaps another time.'

Shortly before eight o'clock the following evening, Mr Windows sat at his harmonium in the empty waiting room, playing Chopin's *Cradle Song* with the expression of a sailor thinking of home. Fay hurried downstairs.

'Cor!' He broke off. 'Doctor, you look dressed to kill.'

She smiled. 'Thank you, Mr Windows. Dr Drake's on duty tonight. She'll he wanting her calls transferred.'

'I hope your evening will prove pleasant, doctor.'

'I hope it will prove sensational. Bye.' She blew him a kiss.

Mr Windows switched to *Just the Way You Look Tonight*. Lucy hurried downstairs.

'Coo!' He stopped. 'Doctor, you could make a whole crew feel they'd been a very long time at sea.'

She smiled. 'Thank you, Mr Windows. Has Dr Liston left? I'm afraid she's in for a dreadfully boring evening at a medical lecture. But I suppose one of us has to keep up to date – professionally, I mean.'

Mr Windows looked puzzled.

'Any calls, Mr Windows, transfer to the Bishop's Arms. They'll find me in the Cordon Bleu room. Dining with Mr Adam Vane.'

'Very good, doctor.'

The front door slammed. He turned back to his harmonium. He blinked. 'The Bishop's Arms?' he muttered. 'The Cordon Bleu room? With Mr Adam Vane? And one said she was attending a lecture...' His cheeks puffed with laughter. 'Straight into the *consommé!*'

He played *La Donna E Mobile, con brio*.

18

'My very best table, monsieur,' said Henri, maître d'hôtel of the Cordon Bleu room, in his rich Gallic accent. 'The spray of flowers, as your secretary ordered on the telephone.' They were orchids in a cellophane box. 'Oh, *merci* monsieur,' he added, bowing low as Adam Vane discreetly passed him a £5 note.

'I want very special service, Henri. This is going to be a very special evening.'

'I understand, monsieur.' Henri tucked the money into the white dinner jacket which he wore with a frilly shirt and a midnight blue velvet bow tie. 'A new – as we say in Paree – *petite poule?* Lady friend,' he explained.

'A very old one.'

'We dance best to familiar tunes,' Henri philosophized, with the air of a *boulevardier*.

'And the music's still playing for me,' said Adam firmly.

'The *carte des vins*.' Henri handed Adam a foot-and-a-half square folder. He dropped his voice. 'I recommend strongly the *Château Chauve-Souris*.'

The Cordon Bleu room was the grillroom of the old coaching inn, newly refitted with gold-fringed hangings, tables with pink cloths and lighting barely strong enough to distinguish the bones in the *truite au bleu*. Mitrebury society agreed that it brought them a garlic-laden whiff of sophistication, that Henri matched the head waiters of Soho, and was entitled to display humiliating French disdain towards any provincial diner failing to overtip him.

'Alfie,' Henri whispered to the pink jacketed young man behind the bar at the dining-room entrance. 'I got some stupid young geezer out there trying to pull a bird. Shove a couple of bottles of the red plonk under the 'ot tap, there's a good bloke. Christ, 'ere comes instant murder,' he added, as Drs Fellows-Smith, Hill and Carmichael appeared from the hotel lobby. '*Bon soir*, messieurs,' he greeted them with Parisian courtesy.

He showed them to a large round table next to Adam's. 'I say,' Freddie declared in a loud whisper as they sat down. 'Isn't that young feller, who's trying to hide behind the wine list, the pimply pill-pusher I set my dogs on, whenever he stuck his shifty face into the surgery?'

'Oh, no,' Roland disagreed. 'He could never afford to eat in a restaurant like this.'

'The place is going down, like everywhere else,' Freddie lamented, glaring towards Adam. 'They'll be letting osteopaths in next.'

'Steady, Freddie.' Roland took the menu from Henri. 'I go to an osteopath about my back. Little Japanese lady. Cracks me, like a lobster claw.'

'A surgeon told me to treat *my* back by sleeping on a board,' Biggin remarked.

'What happened?' Freddie asked.

'Got dreadful splinters.'

'Where's Liz?' asked Roland, looking round.

'What a woman,' Freddie reflected fondly 'I always remember the first time we met. At the point-to-point. She fell, and sustained a black eye.'

'You treated it?' Biggin enquired.

'I applied a beefsteak. Afterwards, we fried and ate it. I have never consumed a morsel so delicious. Wine list, Henri.'

'Certainly, monsieur.' He whipped it from Adam. 'May I recommend the *Château Chauve-Souris*–'

'I wouldn't use it for drenching my donkey in its native Algeria,' Freddie told him. 'It is that spotty quack-medicine hawker.'

173

'Darling doctors–' Liz wore a low-cut scarlet gown, gripping her as closely as a plaster cast. 'Sorry I'm late, but I rather unexpectedly had twins.'

She stopped, staring at Adam. He had the expression of a fox with its eye on a fat rabbit finding itself under the hoofs of the Mitrebury hunt.

'But I know you,' Liz gave a pleasant smile. 'We met a year or so ago.'

'A year or so ago,' Adam agreed uncomfortably.

'She can't possibly know that pharmaceutical costermonger,' Freddie protested.

Liz crossed to Adam's table. 'We ran into one another at St Boniface's Hospital.'

He agreed they had.

'At the dean's delightful cocktail party,' Liz reminisced. Suddenly she recalled, 'It was in the gynaecology finals. I failed you,' she said sharply. 'You knew less about a breech delivery than the Royal Horse Artillery.'

She turned her back. Adam groaned, holding his head. Nothing worse could have happened that evening, he thought sorely. He looked up, and saw Fay standing in front of him.

'Adam! Hi!' She gripped him and kissed him.

'And what,' she heard sternly behind her, 'happened to the lecture?'

She spun round. 'Oh! I couldn't get in. It was overcrowded. Lots of people turned away.'

'A lecture on heavy metal metabolism?' Liz looked amazed.

'Then Adam Vane rang and asked me out to dinner,' Fay continued quickly. 'It was a complete surprise.'

'Absolutely complete.' Adam glanced nervously from Fay to the door.

'I've longed to come here, ever since starting in Mitrebury.' Fay sat. So did Adam. 'I hear the food's terrific. Snails, frogs' legs, flaming pancakes, everything.' She looked startled as Adam jumped up.

'I left the keys in the car,' he explained breathlessly, striding out. He caught Henri in the bar. 'I'm expecting a young lady.'

'But, monsieur, there she is, *voilà*.'

'Another young lady.'

'*Quel homme*,' said Henri admiringly.

'I don't want that young lady to meet this young lady.' He gave Henri another £5.

'*Merci* monsieur. I will detain her here in the bar with a glass of champagne.'

To Adam's alarm, Fay approached from their table. 'Adam sweetie, I fibbed to Lucy about that lecture. I'd feel much happier if she heard of it from me – before she's certainly going to hear of it from that lot.' She jerked her head towards Liz's party. 'And I might be home late?' She smiled meaningfully. 'Mightn't I?'

'She might be out,' Adam suggested distractedly.

'She is, at the Community Health Centre.' Fay felt in her handbag for a coin, 'The poor darling's spending all evening working in the blood bank. Adam!' She stared at him. 'You're shaking. You're not febrile, are you?'

'Just a little allergy. To the smell of garlic. We should have gone somewhere Chinese.'

'Henri,' bellowed Freddie from his table. 'We're starving.'

'*Tout de suite*, monsieur. Impatient bastards,' he added to himself

Adam dazedly followed the head waiter into the restaurant. Fay found the phonebox beyond the bar. He sat down heavily.

'Adam, darling,' called Lucy, waving from the door.

'The blood bank's gone bankrupt, I suppose?' Liz asked.

Lucy put her hand to her mouth. 'Mrs Arkdale! There weren't any donors.'

'How extraordinary! The citizens of Mitrebury are far more generous with their blood than with their gin.'

'Then I had this telephone call from Mr Vane, who was a student with me at St Boniface's. He asked me out to dinner. For old times' sake.'

'I wonder who's looking after the practice?' demanded Freddie loudly.

'Adam!' Lucy stared at him. 'You're shaking. You're having a rigor. Oh, you poor man. I should have you in bed.'

'Doubtless,' said Fay icily, reappearing from the bar.

'What are you doing here?' Lucy demanded angrily.

'And what are *you* doing here, if I may ask?' Fay said tartly.

'Adam asked me to dinner.'

'You are in error. Adam asked *me* to dinner.'

'He most certainly did not.'

'He most certainly did.'

'They do keep repeating themselves,' announced Freddie, his party following the exchanges as though watching a brisk rally at Wimbledon.

'Who *did* you ask to dinner?' Lucy asked Adam furiously.

He gave a weak smile. 'You're both very welcome.'

'I'm not having dinner with *her*,' said Lucy and Fay, pointing at one another.

'I'm going home,' decided Fay.

'So am I,' agreed Lucy.

'You might as well take the orchids,' Adam called after them, handing the box to Henri. 'As they're paid for.'

'Blimey, what a turn-up,' exclaimed Henri confusedly. 'Shall I put them in water?'

Lucy stopped at the door. She gave a sweet smile. 'No,' she said. 'In acid.'

19

'Fay,' said Lucy.

'Lucy dear?' said Fay.

It was eleven-thirty the same evening. The two young doctors were in the sitting-room, sipping mugs of steaming cocoa. The table was strewn with sheets of crumpled, greasy newspaper and the remains of the fish dinner which Mr Windows had compassionately fetched from the Cathedral Chipperie in the High Street.

'I could never have survived Mitrebury without you, Fay.'

'Nor certainly I without you, Lucy.'

'You've been a real friend, ever since we started on the same leg in the anatomy department.'

'Sometimes, Lucy, I've felt as close to you as I've been to any of the men I've been living with. Mind, some of them were stinkers.'

'There are no secrets between us,' Lucy said dreamily.

'Well, none that it's rather fun to divulge.'

'Fay–'

'Lucy?'

'I've something to confess, after that fiasco tonight. When we were all at St Boniface's, and you were away doing your obstetrical course, Adam Vane took me for a week to Sorrento.'

'And when you were away doing your gp course, Adam took me to Torremolinos.'

Lucy glared. 'Sorrento is up-market.'

'Yes, sweetie. But he took me for a whole fortnight.'

'Why didn't you tell me this before?' Lucy snapped.

'Because you'd be unbearable to live with. You're so jealous.'

'I am *not* jealous.'

'And argumentative with it.'

'I am *not!*'

'Hippocrates, Hippocrates,' said Fay wearily. The telephone rang in the waiting-room.

'I'll answer it,' said Lucy briefly. 'I'm on duty, and Mr Windows is pissed.'

Fay reached for her paperback. She read three pages, before becoming aware of Lucy still speaking to someone. Curious, she followed her.

'Very well, I'll be along as soon as I can.'

Lucy put the telephone down. 'It's Mr Fanshawe,' she announced to Fay anxiously. 'He's developed acute abdominal symptoms.'

'Such as?'

'Violent epigastric pain. Apparently he fainted.'

'Vomiting?'

'Some.'

'Diarrhoea?'

'No. And his waterworks are okay.'

'Looks like a perforated peptic ulcer.'

'An ulcer that I missed diagnosing this morning,' Lucy conceded glumly.

'Mind, he is a hypochondriac,' Fay pointed out more cheerfully.

'Even a hypochondriac is entitled to be ill. I'd better hurry across.' Lucy grabbed her medical bag. 'He'll probably need an emergency op at the Infirmary.'

Five miles along the London road, a sign in Lucy's headlights directed her down a winding lane between high grassy banks and thick hedges, which opened abruptly into a saucer containing the village of Fenny Bottom. Under a stone bridge ran the river Wychley, the contents of which Freddie Fellows-Smith painstakingly tried to transfer to his deep-freeze. The village was a row of shops, the Goat and Bees, a pillar-box and a telephone kiosk. Beyond, a narrow track led to a cluster of cottages. Lucy stopped at one she assessed as costing more to redecorate than to buy. It was thatched, timbered, its pretty pink flowers shining in the upstairs lights of the neighbours, close against the fence.

The front door with a heavy cast-iron knocker stood ajar. The house was in darkness. She nervously went inside. A streak of light showed under a door leading from the small, shadowy hall. She raised the latch. The low room had a highly polished floor, beams in the ceilings and walls, a brick fireplace, a chintz sofa and an armchair in which Terry Fanshawe sat in pyjamas and silk kimono reading the *New Statesman*.

'Well!' she exclaimed peevishly. 'You *have* made a quick recovery.'

'But, doctor, I've still the pain.' He rubbed his midriff. 'Thank God the agony has gone.'

She slammed her bag on an oak gate-legged table. 'What of those other symptoms you complained about, over the phone?'

'They seem to have passed off, doctor,' he said mildly. 'I'm sorry to have called you so late, but I was alarmed. Being here all alone.' Lucy looked surprised. 'My wife's in Paris for the night.' He smiled faintly. 'Living it up with a bunch of travel salesmen.'

'I'd better examine you,' Lucy decided. It was still possible he had a leaking ulcer, or perhaps an acute appendix. Not to examine him would leave her open to charges of malpractice. 'Lie on the sofa,' she commanded.

He slipped his kimono from his bare chest. As Lucy pulled down the top of his pyjama trousers to inspect his abdomen, he remarked, 'May I say that the doctor looks dishy tonight?'

'I had a date.'

'Lucky feller.'

'Your tummy's perfectly soft. There's no need for an operation.' She gave the skin a slap as she straightened up.

'That's a relief.' She tossed him his kimono from the chair.

'You knew perfectly well there was nothing seriously wrong – didn't you?'

'I suppose so,' he admitted.

She suddenly felt sorry for him. Like many men successful women attach to themselves, he had the vulnerability of a child.

'It's stupid, but I hate being here alone,' he confessed. 'It's always happening. Greta has to travel a lot, naturally. She just leaves me with something to eat – like a dog. Tonight, it got so unbearable, and I kept thinking how nice you were yesterday at the surgery...'

'If people called the doctor because they felt lonely, we shouldn't have time to treat the sick,' Lucy said primly.

'I'm sorry,' he apologized. 'But as you are here, can I give you a drink to make up for your trouble?' She shook her head. 'Well, can I show you my paintings?' he asked with a smile. 'They may be poor things, but I don't get much chance of displaying them to an intelligent audience.'

'All right,' she agreed after a moment. It seemed a simple way to please him.

He opened the door of his glass-roofed studio, built on the back of the cottage. A canvas stood half-finished on the easel, others were hung or stacked round the room, amid the jumble of paints and brushes and messy rags.

'Why, these are awfully good,' she exclaimed.

'That's kind.'

'I'm not paying empty compliments. I wanted to be a painter myself. But my family pushed me into medical school instead of art school.'

'Really?' he said eagerly. 'That explains it. It's because you're artistic, I took to you.'

The paintings were clowns, fireworks, spiky nudes, white-walled southern towns, bright blue seas with hard-edged white sails. Nothing of the soft beauty of the English countryside through the window, Lucy reflected. The style was forceful and masculine. Was painting his psychological compensation for an overbearing wife?

'They strike me as a combination of Dufy and Buffet,' she told him.

He looked delighted. 'You know, that's something I've always felt myself.'

'Do you sell any?'

'Shall we say, I'm waiting to be discovered? Like a needle in the artistic haystack. I don't despair. Lowry had to wait till middle age. Many had to wait until they were dead. How about that drink, anyway?'

'Okay,' she agreed. He was pleasant. It was preferable to conversing with Fay. After Adam, any man's attentions were a restorative.

He produced a bottle in the sitting-room. 'Try some Sambuca. An Italian liqueur. My wife's duty frees. She always brings me a little present.'

'Your marriage–' Lucy ventured. 'Is it difficult to hold together?'

'Not in the slightest. It's glued by Greta's

money.' He poured two small glasses. 'There's one thing you could do, Lucy – we're not on professional terms now, are we?'

'Of course not, Terry.'

'Which would give me enormous pleasure.' He grinned. 'Don't get alarmed. Let me sketch you. You've got a fascinating face.'

'But I must get back to the surgery. I might have other calls. Anyway, I must go to bed some time.'

'It won't take long. Honestly,' he pleaded.

'Oh, okay,' she said again. 'Perhaps I can hang it in the surgery, instead of the stag's head?'

20

Towards noon the following morning, Mr Windows was soothing himself by playing *Land of Hope and Glory* on the harmonium, when Greta Fanshawe strode through the front door with a rolled sheet of paper.

'Where's Dr Drake?'

He rose with dignity. 'Has madam an appointment?'

'I don't need one.' She brushed past him to Lucy's consulting room, where she was discussing with Fay the borough surveyor's spine on his x-rays.

'Good morning, Dr Drake,' Greta started briskly. 'Thank you for attending my husband last night.'

'Luckily there was nothing wrong.' Lucy looked concerned at her expression.

'There was a lot wrong. You arrived at my house at twelve minutes to twelve. You were seen off by my husband – very affectionately, in his pyjamas – at six minutes past two.'

'How do you know that?' she asked, startled.

'From my neighbour. The bishop's chaplain, the Revd Arthur Dawney.'

'Who I was treating for insomnia,' exclaimed Fay. 'If only I'd given him some real knock-out drops!'

'But, Mrs Fanshawe – I only let your husband sketch me. When he's finished it, I'm going to put it in the waiting-room.'

'I'm sure your patients will find it appropriate,' she said furiously, unrolling a charcoal sketch of Lucy nude, full frontal.

'That's a work of pure imagination!' Lucy snapped.

'That is no excuse. Not to anyone aware of Terry's reputation. And no one is more aware of it than I am. God knows how many of those chits at the art college he's had. And half the shop girls and barmaids of Mitrebury, I shouldn't wonder.'

'Mrs Fanshawe,' said Lucy in exasperation. 'You're fantasizing. Terry simply isn't the sex-mad type.'

'That's something you can argue before the General Medical Council, Dr Drake. Oh, yes, I'm a woman of the world, I know my rights. Nor am I overawed by self important bodies. I intend reporting you for professional misconduct. I am instructing my solicitors in London to start proceedings immediately. I'm aware that a charge against a female doctor is unusual. But women who enjoy men's privileges and men's pay must expect men's penalties.'

She threw the drawing on the desk and marched out.

'Oh, Lucy!' said Fay.

'But absolutely nothing happened,' Lucy protested.

'Nothing?'

'I had a drink and looked at his paintings.'

'You mean etchings?'

'This is no time for medical student humour,' Lucy said angrily.

'Did he kiss you?'

'Of course not. Well. Perhaps, when I left.'

'Oh, Lucy!'

'I was upset about Adam Vane.'

'So was I. But I didn't go out looking for men in pyjamas.'

'You're not being in the slightest helpful. This could he dreadfully serious.'

'She won't go through with it.'

'She will. That woman's got "bitch" stamped right through her, like "Brighton" in a stick of rock.'

'The General Medical Council's much more lenient these days,' Fay said consolingly. 'After all, the gas man's as often alone with a young and sexy housewife as the doctor is.'

'Yes, but she doesn't have to take her clothes off to let him read her meter.'

They fell silent.

'Oh, Lucy,' said Fay sorrowfully.

'Please *don't* keep saying "Oh, Lucy". Can't you be constructive? Whatever Mrs Fanshawe does, my reputation is at stake. Which means the reputation of the practice, too. You're involved as much as I am.'

'Of course I'm not,' Fay objected. 'I've always taken the greatest pains, keeping my nose clean in Mitrebury.'

'You're being smug.'

'I'm not.'

'Yes, you are.'

'I am not.'

'Who's argumentative now?' Lucy demanded.

'Oh, Hippocrates,' Fay said crossly.

They looked at each other. Lucy snapped her fingers. 'Liz Arkdale!'

'She's operating at the Infirmary. Let's phone her,' said Fay eagerly.

Lucy hesitated. 'Is it fair to involve her?'

'Was it fair to involve St George with the dragon? She'll give us the same response.'

At that moment, in the palace on the far

side of the close, the chaplain tapped on the bishop's door and interrupted him talking to Archdeacon Bellwether.

'Will you excuse me, Peter? I was hoping that a chance might offer itself to impart something of importance.'

'Please do,' Mr Bellwether volunteered heartily. The bishop was making enthusiastic plans for his television show. Mr Bellwether had a deepening horror that the bishop intended him to appear in it, exactly as he had ordered him on a lethal diet. 'I must be getting home for lunch. I'm sure the performance will be splendid, Peter, and you will soon be as famous throughout the land as that argumentative chap with the glasses and bow tie.'

'It is my duty to tell you, too, Bill,' the chaplain said. 'As you are a patient of the Old Chapterhouse Surgery.'

'What's wrong with it?' Mr Bellwether demanded shortly. 'They are two extremely able young ladies. They did my injured leg the world of good. Though it is not right yet, not by a long chalk,' he directed to the bishop, clutching himself round the calf

'The reason for my objection is not medical, but moral.'

'Moral?' The bishop's bar of eyebrow

creased in a frown.

'You haven't heard, Peter? Obviously. You know Mrs Fanshawe?'

The bishop nodded.

'She is my neighbour at Fenny Bottom,' the chaplain continued. 'Her father was, of course, a distinguished Mitrebury resident, and a considerable benefactor to the cathedral. Mrs Fanshawe is reporting Dr Drake to the General Medical Council, for professional misconduct with her husband.'

The bishop stared at the chaplain. The archdeacon stared at the bishop. He recalled a line of Trollope's – 'The bishop did not whistle; we believe that they lose the power of doing so on being consecrated.' The Bishop of Mitrebury looked within a whisker of going, 'Cor'.

'What a bizarre situation,' the bishop exclaimed. 'Though I suppose only to be expected, in these days of sexual equality.'

'I refuse to believe it,' said the archdeacon stoutly.

'I am sorry you think me capable of passing on untruths,' the chaplain returned.

'How tragic for the young doctor,' said the bishop. 'Is she the one who doesn't wear the whatever it is?'

The chaplain shook his head. 'How tragic

for Mrs Fanshawe, surely? She has not herself enjoyed good health. Her devotion to her father's business obviously leaves ample opportunity for a husband to philander.'

'If there is a word of truth in it,' the archdeacon continued forcefully. 'I'll bet the blame lies on *that* weak-kneed weasel.'

'Possibly,' said the bishop. 'But he doesn't happen to he responsible for his actions to the General Medical Council.'

'It's most unfair,' snorted the archdeacon.

The chaplain leant over the desk. 'So unusual a case, involving so attractive a lady doctor, will attract wide publicity when it comes for trial in London. I fear that Mitrebury will get a bad press.'

'I hadn't thought of that,' said the bishop.

'Do you remember, Peter,' the chaplain continued eagerly, 'the sad case of the bus shelter? The Bishop's Arms was filled for weeks with dreadful men and women from Fleet Street, all trying to prove us a seething cauldron of vice.'

'That would be most unfortunate, with the TV show coming up,' the bishop admitted. 'We must project a constant image of sanctity.'

The chaplain pressed tighter against the desk. 'Do you not think, Peter, that you might arrange for the two young ladies to leave Mitrebury as soon as possible?'

The bishop's eyebrow creased again. 'But the medical arrangements in Mitrebury are no more concern of mine than those of the bus company.'

'You may not perhaps know, Peter, the appointment of those two doctors was most irregular.' The chaplain lowered his voice. His veins felt the heady surge of power. 'The posts were neither advertised, nor filled, according to regulations laid down for the conduct of our Health Service. I have heard as much from several practitioners in Mitrebury. They strongly resented two young women being forced among them through the back door.'

'I really cannot believe that,' objected the bishop. 'The barriers of modern bureaucracy are difficult to scale and impossible to circumvent. They run from one horizon of our life to the other. It's Bill's committee—'

'It was something to do with Mrs Arkdale.'

'Then I can believe it,' he said.

The chaplain relaxed. He stood up, buttoning his well-pressed, threadbare black coat. 'My own thoughts are perfectly clear. It would be in the best interests of Mitrebury and the young ladies themselves, if they left us before St Bartholomew's Day, if not before the Feast of the Transfiguration, which is next week.'

'Your thoughts are un-Christian, uncharitable and ungallant,' said Mr Bellwether, rising.

The chaplain looked shocked.

'Bill...' murmured the bishop gently.

'You are hounding these two girls, Dawney, when nothing whatever has been proved against either of them.'

'The charge is surely enough, from one so respectable as Mrs Fanshawe.'

'Rubbish. You are trying to rid us of two doctors far too proficient for a place so far off the medical map. You should be applauding Mrs Arkdale's ingenuity in bringing us their benefit. Instead of implying that she has committed some sort of public corruption.'

'Corruption is inexcusable for any benefit,' said the bishop, sternly.

Mr Bellwether drew himself up. 'My lord,' he thundered. 'I am not prepared to start a discussion on ethics. I should prefer to use this moment for informing your lordship that in foisting your insane views about health on us all, your lordship is succeeding in incurring the hostility and, what is worse, the ridicule of the entire Mitrebury clergy. Even more readily than by your lordship's unremitting publicity campaign, selling Christianity like soap and yourself like Mickey Mouse.'

'You must not address the bishop like that, Mr Archdeacon,' said the chaplain angrily.

Mr Bellwether's eye swivelled. 'As for you, Dawney, you are a beastly slacker and scrim-shanker, who avoids the slightest physical exertion, or even discomfort, by pleading sickness.'

'How dare you! I suffer from my heart and my duodenum. Quite tragically.'

'There's nothing much wrong with either organ.'

'And how might you know?'

'Because Mr Windows let me see your medical record card across at the surgery. I apologize for my testiness, my lord. Perhaps I have not recovered from your lordship's Lenten diet, which was not conducive to good temper. Praise God I've seen the light, before ending as a sanctimonious physical wreck.'

He left.

21

At six o'clock that evening, Liz Arkdale screeched in her Ferrari to the front door of the Old Chapterhouse Surgery. Greta and Terry Fanshawe were waiting on a pew.

'So good of you to meet me here,' said Liz to Greta.

'It is nothing, when my happiness is at stake,' she exclaimed dramatically.

'Where are the doctors, Mr Windows?' He was sitting at his desk with heightened dignity for the occasion. 'In the sitting-room? Let's go in.'

Fay sat morosely on the pouffe. Lucy stood by the fireplace, hands clasped knuckle-white.

'I suggested we met so you would all know exactly what will happen at the General Medical Council,' Liz began in a businesslike way. She took the leather armchair, motioning the Fanshawes to the sofa. 'You will make a charge, Greta. You will have to prove it, on the evidence of Mr Dawney. Then both sides will produce character witnesses.'

Terry grinned. 'I might find that difficult.'

'Be quiet,' snapped Greta.

'You realize, the charge is rather more serious than lifting a tin of baked beans from a supermarket?' Liz asked her.

'If I did not think so, I should not be bringing it.'

Liz nodded slowly. 'Very well. You say Dr Drake committed misconduct with your husband last night? Dr Drake denies it. Who is telling the truth?'

'I always tell the truth,' Terry asserted. 'I was in Mr Dawney's Bible class as a teen-ager.'

'I should prefer first-hand evidence.' Liz asked him coldly, 'Did you kiss her?'

'Yes.'

'Well, Dr Drake?' Lucy said nothing.

'I see,' Liz resumed. 'Were any clothes removed?'

'Of course there weren't,' Lucy said shortly.

'There were,' countered Terry.

'You liar,' Lucy exclaimed.

'But, doctor,' Terry asked, 'don't you remember handing back my kimono?'

'The whole charge is a frame-up,' Lucy exploded. 'You people in Mitrebury are utterly mad.'

'Well, the place was cursed by a mediaeval witch,' Terry remarked.

'They burnt her at the stake, too,' Liz reminded him. The door opened. In came the three old doctors.

'Why, it's Liz,' said Biggin Hill in surprise. 'And the Fanshawes. Haven't seen you since the hunt ball.'

'Just come to look up that Bradshaw continental timetable,' Freddie announced. 'The one we kept for years in the bookcase. Shouldn't think the times of the trains have changed much, except to get slower.'

'The fact is, we've decided that after thirty-five years of looking down throats and up – er, things, we need some culture,' Roland explained. 'We thought we'd try Padua.'

'Make a penitential pilgrimage to the famous anatomy theatre in the university there,' Freddie rumbled, 'Where the great Versalius taught. I rather owe it to his ghost, as I somehow managed to pass my anatomy exam without dissecting more than a foot, half an arm, and those sticky bits round the liver.'

'We're going to stay nearby in Venice.' Biggin took the thick, paper-covered timetable from the shelf. 'In Italy, you know,' he added to Greta.

'I am aware of the fact,' she told him bleakly.

'Please carry on what you're doing, whatever it is,' Roland invited. 'We'll be quiet as mice.'

'As you've taken the trouble to come, perhaps we'd better,' Liz decided, turning to Greta. 'I'm sure that Drs Fellows-Smith, Carmichael and Hill will preserve complete professional secrecy about anything they might happen to overhear.'

'We could go to Venice via Vienna by the Orient Express,' Roland suggested, peering through his new glasses.

'That was cancelled two years ago,' Greta said curtly.

'Or direct from Calais, changing at Basle,' Roland continued. 'Though we'd have to scamper, there's only two minutes between trains.'

'I know! Why not put ourselves in the hands of Perkins Travel?' Biggin suggested.

'A smart firm,' Freddie agreed gruffly.

'Very smart,' Roland concurred crisply. 'Remember when they got away with that illegal currency deal?'

Greta sat bolt upright.

'Funny the bank manager should be one of our patients,' Freddie reflected.

'Splendid new office block they've built,' Biggin mentioned. 'Though it does ruin the view of the cathedral from the bridge.'

Roland stared thoughtfully at the ceiling. 'Wasn't there something odd about the planning permission?'

'Nothing odd in the slightest,' Freddie told him. 'Straightforward bribery.'

'That's another strange thing,' Biggin reminisced. 'The councillor involved being one of our patients.'

'Stop it,' snapped Greta.

'Would never have happened when the old man ran the firm,' Freddie continued. 'Now he gave me a month's free fishing in Norway. Magnificent salmon water. Just for persuading a psychiatrist to say his young daughter shouldn't be charged with shoplifting from Harrods.'

'Shut up!' screamed Greta.

'Remember the time she thought herself six weeks pregnant?' Roland remarked. 'An odd fancy to entertain, as her husband was just finishing a six-month exchange job in America.'

'What's this?' demanded Terry furiously, jumping up.

'Nothing, nothing,' Greta murmured. 'You're overreacting.'

'I am? What about you and Dr Drake? Nothing in the slightest nasty happened. Of course it didn't.'

'Then why didn't you tell me that in the first place?' she asked angrily.

'Because you never believe the truth when you don't want to. I'm scared of you, it's my basic trouble,' he burst out. 'I'd say anything to please you. Otherwise you might throw me out. I have to eat, even if it's the horrible little dog's dinner you leave me in the freezer, when you're on the champagne and caviar anywhere from Spain to Singapore.'

She switched her glare to the three old doctors. 'Those remarks were highly unprofessional.'

'But a lot of fun,' Freddie told her amiably.

'Such a pity if they got round Mitrebury,' Liz sighed.

'Not to mention bad for business,' Roland pointed out.

'May I offer some professional advice?' Liz asked sweetly. 'That we *all* develop total amnesia for the period starting at midnight and ending now?'

Freddie added to Greta in a fatherly voice, 'Why don't the pair of you make it up with second honeymoon? Somewhere romantic. Like Bangkok. After all, you get cheap rates,' he pointed out.

'As you're here,' Biggin added, 'perhaps you could fix a cheap package for all three of us to Venice? I seem to remember from an Italian POW – charming chap, damn shame they weren't on our side – that the Canal View Hotel was excellent.'

Greta rose. 'It fell into the canal in 1948. Come, Terry. There is no Mafia like the medical Mafia.'

Grabbing his hand like a child, she hurried him towards the door.

'I take it you're dropping the charges?' Liz called after her.

Greta nodded curtly.

'And you might mention to the Revd Arthur Dawney, that it is extremely un-Christian to covet your neighbour's private life.'

The door slammed. Liz and the three old doctors burst into laughter.

'What a relief!' Lucy was hugging Fay. 'What a terrific slice of luck that our wonderful predecessors happened to drop in.'

'Luck?' said Liz. 'Really, I'm insulted. Do you imagine the four of us didn't work it out to the last sentence this afternoon, while Freddie was hosing down his pigs?'

'Oh! Mrs Arkdale. How can we thank you

enough?' Fay gasped.

'By listening calmly to what your three senior colleagues are now about to say.'

The old doctors looked at each other in embarrassment.

'Go on, Freddie,' urged Biggin.

'You tell them, Roland,' he said evasively.

'You lost the toss,' Roland pointed out.

'Oh, all right.' Freddie gave a nervous cough. 'We had luncheon together at the Bishop's Arms.'

He stopped. 'Good,' said Fay.

'It was what the bloody politicians call a working lunch. We have a little proposition.'

He stopped again.

Roland interrupted. 'We can't express even an atom of our gratitude for your taking this practice off our hands.'

'Taking it by the scruff of its neck, to shake out the moths and cobwebs,' Biggin observed.

'But it hasn't done *us* much good,' Freddie said gloomily. 'We thought life would be glorious when we retired. I'd shoot. Roland had his golf. Biggin could take his car to pieces and put it together again, as he always seems to be doing. Instead of which, we're bored stiff.'

'So you want to come back?' Lucy asked

at once.

Freddie blew his nose. 'You must have heard in Mitrebury that old Lady Beckenham left me a packet? We have completely disrupted your careers. And we may have landed you in trouble with the Health Service, if that ass Dawney wants to make a fuss–'

'I overplayed my hand at that committee,' Liz said guiltily. 'Though I'm sure Dawney *won't* make a fuss. Not about anything. Greta can be relied upon to fix that, with her customary efficiency.'

'For all of which, I should be delighted to write you a cheque in compensation,' Freddie declared. 'Just say how much you'd like.'

'Plus a free ticket to anywhere in the world you wanted a holiday,' Biggin added.

'Not through Perkins Travel,' Liz said quickly.

'Los Angeles,' Lucy announced. She turned to Fay. 'I had a letter from dear Roddy yesterday. He wants his cricket bat in California. And he wants me to bring it. I didn't tell you, because I felt I just couldn't go. It would be letting you down.'

'A ticket to London will do me,' said Fay. 'I had a letter from St Boniface's this morning. The feller doing that haematology research job has got a scholarship to Harvard, and they want me to take it.'

'Splendid,' declared Liz. 'And you've had a taste of general practice, which will leave its flavour for the rest of your professional lifetimes. I've only one regret. You found Mitrebury so dull.'

They became aware of Mr Windows' raised voice in the waiting-room. The door flew open.

'Dr Liston!' A pretty woman of Fay's age stood holding up a stethoscope. 'Is this yours?'

'Oh, my new Japanese transistorized stethoscope,' Fay said delightedly. 'I've been looking for it everywhere.'

'I expect you have. What exactly was it doing at the bottom of my husband's bed?'

'Oh, Fay!' said Lucy.

The publishers hope that this book has given you enjoyable reading. Large Print Books are especially designed to be as easy to see and hold as possible. If you wish a complete list of our books please ask at your local library or write directly to:

Dales Large Print Books
Magna House, Long Preston,
Skipton, North Yorkshire.
BD23 4ND

This Large Print Book, for people
who cannot read normal print,
is published under the auspices of

THE ULVERSCROFT FOUNDATION

... we hope you have enjoyed this book.
Please think for a moment about those
who have worse eyesight than you ...
and are unable to even read or enjoy
Large Print without great difficulty.

You can help them by sending a
donation, large or small, to:

**The Ulverscroft Foundation,
1, The Green, Bradgate Road,
Anstey, Leicestershire, LE7 7FU,
England.**
or request a copy of our brochure for
more details.

The Foundation will use all donations
to assist those people who are visually
impaired and need special attention
with medical research, diagnosis
and treatment.

Thank you very much for your help.